The Secret

W9-BZT-792

"Daddy's son-in-law," said Lynn, "has to be a combination of Jesus Christ, Donald Trump, and General Schwarzkopf, and he can't be seven years older than I am . . . Gary?"

"What?"

"His hands tremble when I touch him."

"Neat," I said.

"He calls me Ling. Nobody's ever called me by a special name. Sometimes he calls me Lingerling."

I had to look away from her face.

"I've never been in love. I'm just so happy."

"Good. That's good."

"So could you handle the Bobby thing for me? Somehow?"

"You mean tell him?"

"You can't say who it is. Not to anyone, Gary."

"You mean write him and tell him you're in love with someone?"

"Don't you think so? Before he comes home and . . ."

Books by M. E. Kerr

Dinky Hocker Shoots Smack!
Best of the Best Books (YA) 1970–83 (ALA)
Best Children's Books of 1972, *School Library Journal*
ALA Notable Children's Books of 1972

If I Love You, Am I Trapped Forever?
Honor Book, *Book World* Children's Spring Book Festival, 1973
Outstanding Children's Books of 1973, *The New York Times*

The Son of Someone Famous
(An Ursula Nordstrom Book)
Best Children's Books of 1974, *School Library Journal*
"Best of the Best" Children's Books 1966–1978, *School Library Journal*

Is That You, Miss Blue?
(An Ursula Nordstrom Book)
Outstanding Children's Books of 1975, *The New York Times*
ALA Notable Children's Books of 1975
Best Books for Young Adults, 1975 (ALA)

Love Is a Missing Person
(An Ursula Nordstrom Book)

I'll Love You When You're More Like Me
(An Ursula Nordstrom Book)

Gentlehands
(An Ursula Nordstrom Book)
Best Books for Young Adults, 1978 (ALA)
ALA Notable Children's Books of 1978
Best Children's Books of 1978, *School Library Journal*
Winner, 1978 Christopher Award
Best Children's Books of 1978, *The New York Times*

Little Little
ALA Notable Children's Books of 1981
Best Books for Young Adults, 1981 (ALA)
Best Children's Books of 1981, *School Library Journal*
Winner, 1981 Golden Kite Award, Society of Children's
Book Writers

What I Really Think of You
(A Charlotte Zolotow Book)
Best Children's Books of 1982, *School Library Journal*

Me Me Me Me Me: Not a Novel
(A Charlotte Zolotow Book)
Best Books for Young Adults, 1983 (ALA)

Him *She Loves?*
(A Charlotte Zolotow Book)

I Stay Near You
(A Charlotte Zolotow Book)
Best Books for Young Adults, 1985 (ALA)

Night Kites
(A Charlotte Zolotow Book)
Best Books for Young Adults, 1986 (ALA)
Recommended Books for Reluctant YA Readers, 1987
(ALA)

Fell
(A Charlotte Zolotow Book)
Best Books for Young Adults, 1987 (ALA)

Fell Back
(A Charlotte Zolotow Book)
Finalist, Edgar Allan Poe Award, Best Young Adult
Mystery
(Mystery Writers of America)

Fell Down
(A Charlotte Zolotow Book)

Deliver Us From Evie

M. E. KERR
LINGER

HarperTrophy
A Division of HarperCollins Publishers

Linger

Copyright © 1993 by M.E. Kerr
All rights reserved. No part of this book may be used or reproduced in
any manner whatsoever without written permission except in the case of
brief quotations embodied in critical articles and reviews. Printed in the
United States of America. For information address HarperCollins
Children's Books, a division of HarperCollins Publishers, 10 East 53rd
Street, New York, NY 10022.
Typography by Al Cetta
❖

Library of Congress Cataloging-in-Publication Data
Kerr, M. E.
    Linger / M.E. Kerr.
       p.   cm.
    Summary: When his older brother suddenly joins the army and is sent
to the Persian Gulf, sixteen-year-old Gary begins to take a new look at
the restaurant that has been the focal point of his family and their small
Pennsylvania town.
    ISBN 0-06-022879-2. — ISBN 0-06-022882-2 (lib. bdg.)
    ISBN 0-06-447102-0 (pbk.)
    [1. Brothers—Fiction   2. Persian Gulf War, 1991—Fiction.
3. Restaurants—Fiction.]   I. Title
PZ7.K46825Li   1993   92-30988
[Fic]—dc20   CIP
                                                                      AC
First Harper Trophy edition, 1995.

FOR VIVIAN SCHULTE
longtime friend and favorite poet
with love

Time is slow, do not go
From here.
And the scheme is a dream
In here.

So linger awhile, let's see that smile,
Secrets are mysteries still.
You'll have your way, you will.

—"Linger" by Jules Raleigh

1

*How would you feel about having a Gulf soldier for a
pen pal?* my brother wrote to Lynn Dunlinger.

If the answer is no, don't write back.

Lynn came up to me near Christmas, at the employees' party Linger always held.

That was when she told me about it.

She said, "Gary? Guess who I got a letter
from! Your brother!"

"Bobby?" I said. I only had one brother. But I
couldn't believe it: Bobby writing Dunlinger's
daughter! He'd never mentioned *that* in his letters home.

"Yes, Bobby! I'm the only girl at Faith Academy who's heard from a serviceman in the Gulf!"

"He's the only one from Berryville to be over
there."

"And the only Linger alumnus. Daddy's real proud of Bobby."

"*Now*," I said. Lynn ignored my sarcasm. Since she went away to school and wasn't around the restaurant that much, maybe she didn't know Bobby'd had a major falling-out with her father. No one but those two knew why but Bobby said he'd never work for Dunlinger again, never set foot inside Linger again, either.

The Dunlingers behaved like parents of the holy child they had to keep safe and sheltered for some special destiny. Lynn couldn't date until she was seventeen, and by that time she was enrolled in a Catholic boarding school ninety miles from Berryville, in the middle of nowhere. If she did date, she had to double date with Gloria Yee, daughter of Lung Yee, Linger's maître d'. Summers Lynn went to a camp called Le Soleil, where they spoke only French.

Take advantage of your advantages, Mr. D. liked to say. I guess that was what my brother was doing.

It'd have to have been a war or something like it to get my brother's toe in Lynn Dunlinger's front door.

I don't know if you remember those days, but there were yellow ribbons hanging off everything, and more flags around than you see on July Fourth.

Who was going to answer that kind of letter saying no, thanks, I'll pass on writing one of you guys?

Preppies and college freshmen from Philadelphia and its outskirts would get in line at holiday time to date Lynn. I never saw her date anyone from Berryville.

Before Saddam Hussein turned the world upside down, no one could have told me the one guy from Berryville Lynn would be bragging wrote her a letter would be my big brother.

At the party I could see Thayer Drake out on the porch waiting for her, his ears red from the cold. He was in his last year at Choate, a little preppy prince in a Paul Stuart tweed suit, a rep tie, and jazzy boots with spurs, long hair tied in back with a silk scarf.

Thayer Drake wouldn't be comfortable coming inside for a drink with the waiters, busboys, cooks, and clerks who worked in the restaurant Lynn's father owned.

The big sign outside said:

LINGER

PROPRIETOR, NED DUNLINGER
ESTABLISHED 1959

Inside there was a smaller sign saying:

YOU DON'T HAVE TO PRAISE US
OR LAUGH AT OUR JOKES.
EAT HEARTY, COME OFTEN,
YOU'RE ONE OF THE FOLKS

Dunlinger said he wanted his customers to feel that Linger was unique, that there was so much more to it than a meal out, with some musician entertaining. . . . He also said his marriage was that kind: unique, much more than he'd expected.

Dunlinger adored Lynn, of course—she was his only child—but he also talked about his wife all the time, in glowing terms. He came off as a romantic character, certainly where Natalia Dunlinger was concerned.

He'd built this special apartment for her at the top of Linger, with a cupola above it, and a small square balcony outside, enclosed with a little white fence.

Mrs. Dunlinger sometimes rested there, or watched the sunset from a white wicker rocker with a glass of champagne. It was her private little area. She called it Lingering Shadows. Sometimes I sneaked up there when I knew she wasn't at the restaurant.

It smelled good there. I knew it was a perfume called Red. I'd seen the bottle in the bathroom. I'd sprayed a little in the air and looked out at the hills of Berryville, and I'd wished I had a great love. Not some dumb little meet-me-by-my-locker thing, but something that would be once-in-a-lifetime, earthshaking, secret, dark, and possibly even deadly.

I would close my eyes and try to imagine the face of this beloved female, but nothing ever came . . . except Lynn Dunlinger. Everyone's Dream Girl. Berryville's one world-class beauty.

And I would tell myself: No Way! . . . Nooooo Way! It wasn't just that I was sixteen and she was seventeen, or that I was a sophomore in high school and she was a senior in boarding school. It was what Bobby always said: Why line up with the sheep and drool over *her*? That's not for the cool, cool Peel brothers! There're a lot of fish in the sea; you just haven't swum from the little pond into the big sea. Wait till you get your butt out of Berryville, Gary—she'll look like nothing to you.

Both our parents thought Berryville was paradise.

They loved Berryville and they loved Linger.

My dad, Charlie Peel, was Linger's manager, and Wanda, my mother, did the books for the place, from home.

Dad thought The Boss hung the moon, and Mom talked about the Dunlingers the way the English rave about The Royal Family: Every little thing they did fascinated her.

It used to embarrass Bobby when he'd fall into the family rut. Working up there as a waiter, same as I did after he joined up, Bobby'd rave about how smart Dunlinger was, then say something to play it down, like "Now I sound like Dad and Mom!"

But Bobby often fought with Dunlinger, too. He hated the way Dunlinger controlled everything about Linger. Bobby griped about the rules, and the way Dunlinger saw that they were followed.

When Mr. Yee sat people in the dining room, he had to seat unattractive customers back by the kitchen doors (unless they were on Dunlinger's A list of old, well-heeled regulars). No men without ties, or ladies in pants, ever in The Regency Room. They went into The Grill, as did customers with children in tow. Jules Raleigh, the musician, had to play upbeat songs until after dinner, when he'd go into The Grill and the bar drinkers would sit around the piano and request blues.

No drunk, ever, no matter who it was, could stay at a table or on a barstool; he or she had to leave. Fresh flowers on the tables, clean windows, and in the smoking section no more than two butts in an ashtray before you emptied it.

There was a long list of rules.

Dunlinger had the only real restaurant in town. The hotel dining room was a tacky place that couldn't keep a cook more than six months. The others were fast-food joints like Waffle Waffle and McDonald's.

Linger paid a lot of attention to Berryville, too.

It wouldn't seem like Christmas in our town without the Linger tree. We all went up there to watch the lights go on and sing carols every December fifteenth . . . Easter there was the egg rolling out on the lawn, for the kids . . . and on the Fourth of July, Linger's fireworks could be seen and heard for miles.

Linger was the best thing about the town. Bobby said it was all due to Dunlinger, until their fight turned Bobby against him.

After that, Bobby joined the Army, and it was as though Linger didn't exist where he was concerned. He never once asked about Linger or the Dunlingers. If we mentioned them during our phone calls, he changed the subject.

But once there was the threat of war, and Bobby was shipped over to Saudi Arabia, once he'd finally swum from the little pond into the big sea, what did he do first thing?

He wrote Lynn.

2

—*from the journal of Private Robert Peel*
Saudi Arabia

First thing at Fort Hood, this black guy in a Smokey the Bear Hat barked out, "On your face!"

I was right off the bus with the other new recruits.

I stared back at him, didn't have a clue what he wanted.

He called himself Kali Andala, black as the Dunlingers' cat, Joan, and just as angry.

Behind me this guy whispered, "He wants you to do push-ups."

"Beat your face, asshole!" Sergeant Andala introduced me to the Army's pretty talk. His lips practically touched mine, he was so close, and I could smell his morning coffee.

I got down and started going. It was just like the old days out behind Berryville High on the football field, the coach barking at me to save some energy because I'd do some laps next.

"I want twenty!" Sergeant Sweet Talk told me.

A guy behind me muttered, "Jesus!" like he felt for me, and the drill sergeant got on his case next.

He said you're going to beat your face, too, greasehead, because the guy behind me was Spanish, and Sergeant Andala liked to call you the worst thing anyone could. (Italians were wops, and he called a German Sauerkraut Breath.)

Next he asked this guy his name, and it went like this:

"Augustin Sanchez, Sir."

"You a little Spic girl from Porto Ricko, Sanchez?"

"No, Sir. I'm a Mexican from New York City."

"You this Yo-Yo Peel's girlfriend?"

"No, Sir, Drill Sergeant! I'm a male, Sir."

10

I was at their feet, up to five and already feeling it.

"You look like a girl or something, a movie star or something, pretty boy!"

"I'm sorry, Sir. I can't help how I look, Sir!"

"You can help how you act, Movie Star."

"Yes, Sir."

"If you ever try again to help out that Yo-Yo down there beating his face, I'll have your ass!"

"Yes, Sir!"

"Now *you* give me fifty, Movie Star!"

"Yes. Sir!"

What is it with me? All I need to do is show up anywhere and someone there will hate me on sight. Dunlinger used to say I had an attitude. He'd say, You could be my younger self with your cocky strut and your smirk. You've got to bury it, kid! Always pretend to be a bigger fool than you are, Smart Guy, or someone's going to nail you.

Movie Star and me are laughing about it now, sitting on a cot near our tank. I never saw so many stars in one sky.

"I only got to do twelve push-ups," Movie Star says. "Then I caved in. You did all twenty."

I tell him I was something of a jock in Berryville High, and not much of a student. One reason I joined up: for the $5,000 bonus, yes, but also for the chance to go to college, since the family savings should go to the brain, not the brawn. I tell him Gary's going to be a lawyer.

Movie Star says he's no jock, but he's got four brothers, so he joined up for the same reasons. He says instead of sports at the school he went to in New York City, he danced.

I tell him Gary and me are the cool, cool Peel brothers. "We don't dance, we don't *have* to."

He says he'll teach me if I don't know how.

I tell him he's too pretty to dance with. I'd get a name dancing with him. We *all* call him Movie Star now.

He calls me Roberto.

I tell him the only word I know in Spanish is Mañana.

I don't tell him that for a while it was a

Mexican restaurant in Berryville. Not long. Not after Dunlinger heard it was doing okay. I don't tell him about the kid named Carlos whose father ran the restaurant. But I think of Carlos every day of my life.

Movie Star sits hugging his knees, socks on his hands because it is so cold. Tomorrow the day's heat will kill us, but at night it is freezing.

Movie Star says if I want to learn more than *mañana*, a good way is to learn a Spanish song.

He sings,

> *"Ya que para despedirme,*
> *Eres tan solo un sueño."*

I copy it down because I like what it says.
It goes,

> *Keep from saying farewell,*
> *For you are only a dream.*

I think of Lynn. Sometimes I wonder if I was fascinated by her just because she was Dunlinger's daughter. I had in my lifetime exactly three conversations with Lynn. One about how Joan holds her bell with one paw when she hunts, and goes on three legs. . . . One about removing the toilet plunger from the downstairs Ladies' after it was plugged up, because it looks bad in there. . . . One about how she bets she will remember Christmas at Linger no matter what any future Christmas is like because her father really knows how to make Linger magic then. Agreed.

I wouldn't mind having a beer, but there's no booze anywhere since it is prohibited in this country. Even *Playboy* is.

We drink Sharp's nonalcoholic beer, not the same and it's usually warm.

Movie Star says, What if the Iraqis decide to lay it on us first, like tonight?

I say, The only thing I'm really afraid of is the mines.

What if they use gas? Movie Star persists.

We got gas masks, I say.

What if it's not that kind? What if it's some new thing that just has to be in the air and your bones turn to jelly?

I change the subject, ask him how often Amy writes.

He says he doesn't get a letter every day but she sends one every day.

"Does your Lynn write every day too?"

I shrug, lie. I got one from her, though. She could have written it to anyone. *Well, tell me what it's like over there* kind of thing.

Off in the distance we see a line of camels moving across the desert on a route marked by cyalume light sticks, the kind I used to keep in the glove compartment of my old Mustang in case I got lucky.

Break it in half and there was this soft little green light girls loved.

Once one said she'd heard about me, that I was just a makeout artist, and she wasn't going to risk getting AIDS.

I had the name but not that big a game.

The girls I really liked I never got the nerve to ask out. So I'd pretend I didn't even see them, or I'd whistle at them through my fingers, like a hardhat, yell out my car window, "Yo! Baby!"

But I never whistled at L.D. I never let on how I felt about her, to anyone. I didn't even tell Gary, though I think he had a crush on her himself.

Down the way someone's playing that song again on Desert Shield Radio, the 91st Psalm.

You will not fear the terror of the night.

I wonder if I'll die without ever knowing what someone like Lynn Dunlinger says when you kiss her.

3

"What did she have on?" my mom said.

"How would I know? This green thing."

"A dress?"

"Yeah, I think."

"She's home for Christmas vacation early this year. Her school's let out early."

"Mom, did you hear what I said? Bobby and her are writing."

"Bobby and *she* are. Who said *she* was? Did she say *she* was writing to *him*?"

"What did you think she'd do? Bobby probably wrote her that he was homesick and he needed a letter."

"Did she *say* she wrote him?" Mom persisted.

I couldn't remember. After she dropped her little bombshell about hearing from Bobby, I was too busy trying to look like that didn't surprise me, that it'd take more than that to turn *me* around.

I told Mom she didn't have to *say* she was writing him. Who wouldn't write him? Have to be an Iraqi who wouldn't, a Russian, not, believe me, a Dunlinger. They had the biggest flag in town, and Mr. Dunlinger was American Legion, Rotary, Lions, go down the lists, he'd be there.

Mom said, "Oh, yes, she would have to say she was writing to him before I'd believe it."

My father piped up then, "*I* believe it! What I have trouble believing is *Bobby* writing *her.* I thought he was through with all Dunlingers forever!"

"I knew Bobby'd never stay mad at Mr. D.," said Mom. "Those two were thick as thieves, never mind their little falling out."

We never knew what it was really about, but there was a rumor around that Bobby and Mr. Dunlinger fought over something to do with a Mexican restaurant called Mañana. It opened down on the canal one summer, and I remember being surprised when Bobby said Dunlinger called the owner a "wetback."

One of Dunlinger's rules at Linger was no one on the staff could make any ethnic slurs, or tell any jokes about minorities, not even gays. He said the only name for anyone who walked through the front door was "customer," and anyway, he always added, I don't like bigotry of any sort!

I'd even heard Dunlinger put them out of business, and that Bobby quit because of it. But that didn't really seem like my brother. Bobby wasn't that kind of hero. He'd mop up the floor with anyone who went after me, and he'd stick by little kids up against a bully, but he'd never been into causes. You can bet he'd never have joined the Army if he'd thought he'd have to fight a war.

My father said, "Well, if Bobby *is* writing Lynn, he's got a lot of competition."

"Like Thayer Drake," I said. "He was waiting for her after the party."

"She dates others like her," said my father. "Home from school for the holidays she gets Gloria Yee and they double date. You know the rules. They're to protect her."

My father seemed pleased at that idea.

Sometimes I couldn't believe Bobby and I were Charlie Peel's kids. He had a slightly wimpy way about him, maybe from years of looking up to Dunlinger, or maybe it was the rimless glasses he wore, and the fact he was mostly always in a suit and tie. He was shorter and thinner than both Bobby and me, too, and his blond hair was gray now and thinning.

We had his blue eyes, but any sparkle reflected in them came from Mom. She kept her hair blond with the help of Clairol, and her spirits high on an overdose of optimism.

You'd see the two of them together, you'd think she hadn't married her first choice and he had.

"Lynn Dunlinger wouldn't be writing Bobby and going with Thayer and the others at the same time, would she?" my mother asked.

Dad heaved a sigh, "She's just *writing* him! Lynn doesn't *go* with anyone. You *know* that, Wanda."

"What exactly did she say?" my mother asked me. "Start from the beginning, and don't leave anything out."

"Okay," I said, "Lynn Wonderful Dunlinger, with her laughing green eyes, in a green silk dress, black shoes, long black hair down her back, breath smelling minty, sidled up to me at the party and saiddddddddddddddd . . ."

My father shot me a look, but my mother was listening as pleased as though I was telling a fairy tale.

"What? Said what exactly? What did she say?"

4

—*from the journal of Private Robert Peel*
Saudi Arabia

She said to look for a Christmas box, but in her letter there is no photo so maybe I never said send one. All the guys seem to have them in their helmets, or in their cammie pockets.

We have moved out of our tanks into four-man tents. We all made a Christmas tree from a camouflage tent suspended from a pole. Hung with all colors of stick lights, looks real authentic from a distance.

We played a little sandlot football, and we've got lots of sand to play in too. It is everywhere, in everything, a fine sand like a ton of talcum powder has been dropped on us.

Movie Star says what he'll miss on Christmas Day is the tamales his mother makes, that she goes all out for the holiday and they have everything Mexican, tortillas and stuff.

His father plays guitar in a group called La Raza and his mom is a school principal. Besides his four brothers he has one little sister.

His girlfriend, Amy, sends him photos of herself and is everything he has bragged that she was and then some!

Her father does not like that Movie Star is chicano.

What is your girlfriend's family like toward you, he wants to know? I tell him no problem. (HA!)

5

Berryville was just a little Pennsylvania town, no more than about eight thousand people, and we all knew everyone's business.

We all knew the only man in town speaking out against our boys going over to defend the Persian Gulf was Mr. Raleigh, the English teacher.

He'd say he was for the boys but against the buildup over there.

He'd wear a yellow ribbon but not a flag.

He'd say when will we ever learn, and he'd say it was going to turn into another Vietnam.

Nights Mr. Raleigh played both piano and violin at Linger. He was divorced and lived at Flynn's boarding house, down near Waffle Waffle, so I suppose he didn't mind being in the restaurant every night. He got a good meal, which meant he

could eat anything from the menu, unlike us gal-
ley slaves who got macaroni and cheese or turkey
hash, or some other leftovers.

He was the youngest teacher at B.H.S.,
twenty-four, and a star swimmer in his college
days, even though one leg was a lot shorter than
the other. On his right foot he had to wear a
heavy, black shoe with a built-up heel, and still
he bobbed when he walked.

In his classroom he'd printed on the chalkboard:

DO SOMETHING ORIGINAL!
SAY SOMETHING PROVOCATIVE!
WAKE UP YOUR PASSIONS!
CHANGE!

One added since the crisis in the Persian Gulf
said:

FEEL FOR OTHER PEOPLE!

The story went that his little boy was almost a
vegetable, institutionalized somewhere, and that
his wife couldn't take it and had run off, leaving
him to cope.

Redheaded, he had cobalt-blue eyes you could

see across a room. He still smoked. Camels, the same stupid brand Mom used to be hooked on. Mr. Dunlinger would give him these little lectures about it. Not lectures about not wanting him to do it in Linger, but ones about not wanting him to die young.

"We like you, Jules," he'd say. "We want you alive."

I always thought Dunlinger missed having a son. First he favored Bobby, then it was Jules Raleigh.

Mr. Raleigh could have passed for his son, too. Dunlinger had the same rugged build, hair that was not red but certainly rust colored, and that sort of tough look to his body and face that Mr. Raleigh had.

If you saw him sitting down, you'd figure Mr. Raleigh for someone who would be out on the football field, not this fiddler standing at a table in The Regency Room, playing "Claire de Lune" while people ate prime ribs.

Sometimes, late at night, in The Grill, Mrs. Dunlinger would go up and whisper something to him, then stand by his piano and sing some of the old, slow songs: something Barry Manilow wrote, or Billy Joel or The Beatles: "Mandy" or

"Leave a Tender Moment," maybe "Yesterday."

Her blond hair was a lot lighter than Mom's, almost white, and she had this high soprano voice you don't expect to hear singing one of those songs. The novelty of it carried her for a while. But most people knew if she wasn't Ned Dunlinger's wife, she wouldn't be up there trilling her heart out. Still, most people liked her. She was one of these "good ole gal" types, someone you'd describe as a good sport, or a good heart—whatever it was, there'd be good in front of it. She liked clothes, and she always looked sexy in these slinky gowns she'd pour herself into weekends, sometimes strolling around with a gardenia pinned to her hair.

Whenever she got up to sing, Mr. Dunlinger always stopped what he was doing and listened, chin in his hand, sometimes eyes a little teary.

You never knew what she'd turn up in, but Mr. Dunlinger wore the same thing every night. A black dinner jacket (white in summer) and black pants. A red rose in his lapel.

He knew everyone by name, knew all the current jokes, never told an off-color one, but always left his customers laughing, even when the joke wasn't that funny. People were somehow delighted by any attempt of his at wit, same as they were when a president would show even the slightest sense of fun, relieved that, after all, he was like everyone else.

My dad'd say, "He's a character, our Mr. D."

"What'd he do now?" My mother'd turn down the sound of the TV with the remote control.

"It's not what he did, it's what he said."

"What?" and there would actually be color coming to her cheeks, excitement starting to dance in her eyes, for it was Dunlinger time, folks!

The old man was about to get out the shaker, pour some whiskey sours, and sit down to talk about THEM.

And I'd be out of there.

That was what was going on this December afternoon a few days before Christmas and a day after the employee party at Linger.

I left the house early and walked up the hill to the restaurant. I'd go in and fool around in the kitchen. Sometimes I'd head up to the lounge, where I'd catch Mr. Raleigh having a smoke, and we'd talk about Bobby. He was always trying to figure out what made Bobby join the Army so suddenly.

I remember once he said, "I never thought Bobby'd put himself in the way of that much control."

"I never thought of it that way," I said. "I don't think Bobby did, either."

"Remember when his hero was James Jones, the writer?"

"Sure. He read everything he wrote. I always thought that's where he got the idea to join the Army."

"I think he was just mad at something," said Mr. Raleigh. "Bobby's not the soldier type. He didn't want to fight like James Jones. He wanted to write like him."

That was long before anything started brewing in the Persian Gulf.

I was thinking about all that late that afternoon just before Christmas—the first one ever without Bobby.

I was tired from basketball practice. Coach had worked our tails off because there was a scout from one of the big three colleges looking over Barley Dicks, our best player.

I decided to get in a nap before I went on duty. As I went up the front walk, I could see that Lingering Shadows was dark. No one knew I went up there. I'd read there, sometimes. There wasn't any TV. I'd read novels and short stories, all kinds. I wasn't like Bobby, who'd narrow in on one writer, read only that one, then swear by him. I liked to skip around. Bobby liked to see if he could write himself. He'd start stories and never finish them.

I sneaked up the stairs, afraid I'd run into someone on staff who'd report me. I was off limits. I wasn't supposed to leave the kitchen/dining room/lounge area.

I was halfway up the steps when I heard Mr. Raleigh's voice coming from Lingering Shadows.

He was saying, "I didn't want this to happen, and we've got to keep it from ever happening again! . . . NO! No! *You* listen to *me!*"

I didn't hang around to hear more.

6

—from the journal of Private Robert Peel
Saudi Arabia

Christmas Eve. Saudi Muslims don't want female entertainers over here unaccompanied by husbands, so Bob Hope drops the Pointer Sisters and Marie Osmond from his Christmas show; only female is Mrs. Hope.

Free everything courtesy of corporate America. Suntan lotion from Avon, disposable cameras from Kodak, golf balls from Wilson, and just in case the Iraqis don't kill us, Phillip Morris sends cigarettes to do it.

I tell Movie Star about Christmas holidays at Linger starting ten days before, when they light the tree. After that, everyone who comes for dinner brings gift-wrapped toys for the kids at Eloise, the children's home. Then on

31

Christmas Eve Dunlinger plays Santa under the tree, passing out stuff to them. We all sing and drink cocoa.

Movie Star says his favorite holiday is *diez de Septiembre*, Mexican Independence Day. It's not for anglos, though, he says. Are there chicanos at this Eloise?

I don't remember. But I think of the Elizondo family again . . . and of Mañana, the reason for the blow-up with Dunlinger, the real reason I am over here.

I think of Carlos Elizondo constantly.

It doesn't have to be a studio photograph, my brother wrote her, *just a snapshot or something so I can remember what you look like. (Just kidding!) . . . You don't have to if you don't want to, but it sure would be nice to see a pretty face besides Movie Star's. Here a woman hides herself under something called a chador. It is like a sheet only it's black and it goes over everything but the eyes. . . . What does your dad think of this war, I wonder, though don't say I asked since it's not my business, but I bet that big flag is out on the front porch.*

I was out of breath from running down the stairs and away from what was going on in Lingering Shadows. The phone was ringing and ringing, so I answered it the way we'd been taught to do.

"Linger. We open at six thirty. May I take your reservation?"

"Who is this?" said a voice that sounded like Mrs. Dunlinger's.

"Gary Peel," I said. "Who is this?"

"This is Mrs. Dunlinger, Gary."

I felt relieved. I'd thought she was back there at the top of the stairs with Mr. Raleigh.

"Where are you?" I asked her.

"Now where would I be at this hour? I'm home, Gary, you know that." The Dunlingers always ate dinner at home.

"Yes, Ma'am. I do know that."

"But I'm looking for Lynn. Have you seen her?"

"No, Ma'am."

I wasn't letting anything register yet. I was only glad that what'd I first thought was going on up in Lingering Shadows wasn't. The Dunlingers were like Ronald and Nancy Reagan or Clair and Cliff Huxtable from the old *Cosby* TV show. If they could play around on each other, then there wasn't any such thing as real romance.

Mrs. Dunlinger said, "Lynn told us not to wait dinner and we didn't, but Lake Budde is calling here every fifteen minutes for her."

Why couldn't they have ordinary names? Why did they always get called things like

Thayer and Lake? There was even an Osborne in that crowd. Osborne de la Marin the Fourth.

"If I see her, I'll tell her, Mrs. Dunlinger."

"We're on our way there, but I don't think she's there if you haven't seen her."

"I haven't, Ma'am."

"Lynn's so popular with all the boys."

"Yes, Ma'am."

"She can have her pick, I guess."

"I guess."

"So . . . how's your brother?" she said next, and I wondered if she'd been sending him a little message with those words, maybe telling him not to get his hopes up.

"He's just waiting to see what's going to happen, over there, I guess," I said.

"Mr. Dunlinger says we're not going to war, don't worry. That Saddam's crazy, but he's not so far gone he won't be interested in saving his own neck."

"Yes, Ma'am."

She was telling me what Mr. Dunlinger said President Bush ought to do when suddenly I saw Lynn.

She slipped out the door that led up to Lingering Shadows, all by herself, all in white, even the high-heeled boots she had on with fur tops above her ankles. She was carrying a white leather jacket with a fur top, too. So much for animal liberation.

I tried to get her eye. I wasn't sure if she wanted to talk to her mother.

"Of course, Mr. D. was like a lot of Americans who thought Saddam was just saber rattling when he was threatening Kuwait. But he'll get out now. Mr. D. says he has no choice."

"I know it," I said, but I was talking through my hat. I didn't even know what was going on over there in the Gulf. I was trying to learn fast, because of Bobby, but it was really hard to understand.

I watched Lynn drop her jacket on the wing chair in the hall and head into The Regency Room in a white miniskirt. It was taking me a long time to admit what was going on around me, mostly because I couldn't believe it.

". . . so don't you worry, Gary," said Mrs. Dunlinger, "Bobby's helping to scare the pants off that bully!"

I thought of the three words Mr. Raleigh wrote on the blackboard the week before, saying

what the whole Persian Gulf crisis was for: ALL
FOR OIL!

When Mrs. Dunlinger finally finished what
she had to say, I told her I'd keep my eye out for
Lynn.

I said I'd tell Lynn that Lake Budde was
burning down the phone wires.

The Regency Room was the number-one dining
room, where everybody who knew anything
about Linger always wanted to sit. We'd put our
old customers in there (see how you get swallowed up in Dunlingerland, saying "we" this and
"we" that?). There's shelves of old books against
a paneled wall, these striped banquettes, the big
crystal chandelier overhead, underfoot a thick
rug you'd want to curl up and sleep on.

Early in the evening, Mr. Raleigh played his
violin in that room, and later he played piano in
the one next to it, The Grill, with plum-shaded
leather chairs, and booths for lovers and people
who didn't think eating out was all about seeing
who was there and calling across stupid things to
them.

The whole Dunlinger family was up on one

wall in oil paint: the grandfather and grand-
mother, then Ned, and Natalia and Lynn. Don't
forget Joan, the black killer cat who spent most
of her life terrifying any creature that came into
Lingering Pines, the small woods behind the
restaurant.

Then I saw Lynn, when I came out of The
Grill. She was at The Market Basket, which was
what the salad bar was called. An enormous basket was suspended from the ceiling, full of raw
vegetables, various greens, macaroni, cole slaw,
mushrooms, the works.

I called over, "Lynn? Your mother says Lake
Budde is calling every fifteen minutes for you."

She was standing there nibbling on a carrot
stick while she filled up a plate with other rabbit
food.

She looked embarrassed. "I could die that she
tells my business all over Berryville."

"She just told *me*," I said.

"If she told you, she'll tell anybody."

She must have seen my face, because she
came rushing over to purr, "I didn't mean it that
way, Gary. That sounded just awful!"

I was beginning to think Mr. Raleigh had

someone else up there, because that was what I wanted to think: that it wasn't Lynn. Her hair was like silk falling to her shoulders, and she was smiling right into my eyes. . . . If war really did break out, maybe she'd even feel bad enough to *marry* Bobby. Or maybe he'd come home this hero she would really fall in love with. I wished Bobby everything good in the world but that.

She was fussing around me, cooing, asking me did I *ever* eat pasta or potatoes or bread? Because she bet not . . . not with my waistline, not with my "skin tone," whatever that meant. She didn't smell of Red. It was something lighter, more like summer flowers.

"I've been meaning to ask you something, Gary. Does your brother like to read Stephen King?"

I told her about his James Jones period, and that I didn't know what came after that, if anything did.

"Who's James Jones?"

"He wrote *From Here to Eternity*."

"I saw that on tape! Burt Lancaster made love to Deborah Kerr on the beach! It was really steamy!"

"I don't remember."

"Then you didn't see it!" She laughed. "Anyway, I sent Bobby the new King in a Christmas box Mom and I packed for him. I sent him some English shaving cream, too, and some aftershave. And a few jars of Planter's nuts, one entirely cashews. I love cashews the best, myself. Does Bobby?"

"I don't know," I said. I didn't. I said, "*I* like them," but she looked past me blankly as though I was the waiter at her dinner party and I'd suddenly made an unwelcome disclosure about my personal tastes.

She put down her plate for a moment and opened the white leather purse she'd hung from her arm.

"I have something for you," she said. "I just love it, but Daddy'd be furious if *I* ever wore it."

I couldn't imagine what she would have for me.

It was a button, large and white with black letters and what was supposed to look like red drops of blood across it.

I'd seen it before on Mr. Raleigh's bulletin board.

We SHELL not EXXONerate Saddam Hussein for

his actions. We will MOBILize to meet this threat to vital interests in the Persian GULF until an AMOCOble solution is reached. Our best strategy is to BPrepared. FINAlly, we ARCOming to kiss your a ——.

"I support the boys," she said, "but not the reason they're over there."

"I don't know too much about it," I said.

I remembered seeing this fifteen-year-old Kuwaiti girl on CNN testifying how she'd seen these babies being taken from their incubators by Iraqi soldiers in Kuwait, who left them on the freezing floor to die.

I'd done a paper on it weeks before.

Lynn handed me the button.

"Your daddy'd be furious if *I* ever wore it, too," I said. "How could I wear it anyway, with Bobby over there?"

"Of all people, you should wear it. Do you want your brother to go to war for Exxon, Gary?"

I wanted to ask her since when was she this big peace activist? But I knew the answer had to do with whatever was going on up in Lingering Shadows with Mr. Raleigh.

So I just said, "Bobby joined the Army. He

41

knew he wasn't signing on with a rock and roll band."

Then she said something that really surprised me. She put the button back in her bag as she said it, not looking at me. "That was you on the stairs, wasn't it?"

"Yes," I said.

She waited until she had the bag back on her arm. Then she raised her eyes and for a second met mine.

She said softly, "Don't tell anyone, Gary."

"I won't," I said.

8

Christmas Day. With the mail comes the announcement we're moving north tomorrow.

I have to leave everything behind since we lug around gas masks and protective gear. I've never read Stephen King, but the novel weighs about five pounds. . . . I put on something she sent called Elite by Floris, an after-shave "balm," and the guys call out, Who's the whore in the tent?

This tent is unheated, sleeps twenty (two women). I'm in a bag on top of a cot.

Now I wish I'd brought all the Planter's nuts, but I only dumped some cashews in my pocket.

We are deeper in the desert now, and believe it or not the food is improving. Had T rations, turkey with gravy that tasted like a Swanson's frozen dinner, but at least it was hot, not like the MREs, so-called Meals Ready to Eat. Ready for who to eat? is the question.

Now we got new visitors. These Bedouins pass through with their camels and goats. Nomadics don't live in one place ever. Other newcomers are scorpions and sand vipers. Would you believe chickens? We've got them!

The reason for the chickens is they're backups to our gas-monitoring machines. The machines are supposed to sound if there's any chemicals, but in case they don't, the chickens go belly up.

Now I know I never knew what lonesome was. Think of how I'd sit around home with MTV on, drinking a cold Coke in my Jockeys, chewing on a Milky Way. Not sure now I didn't die pushing my Musty up to ninety, and this is hell. Sitting here in the long underwear Mom sent me, dreaming of nothing more special than a hot shower, sand behind the crystal of my Timex, underneath my fingernails, toenails, probably in my brain . . . and over the radio, Baghdad Betty is telling us our sweet-hearts are sleeping with Tom Cruise, Arnold Schwarzenegger, and Bart Simpson!!! (Have a cow, G.I.!)

You'd think they'd check stuff out before they broadcast it. Be funny if anything was funny here.

Movie Star found some guy here who actually lived in Kuwait when he was a kid. He's from Boston, a Corporal Sweet we call Sugar. He knows a lot about music, wants to write music, be a new Axl Rose or a Garth Brooks.

His father's in the petrochemical industry, and he's been all over the Middle East.

He says the only way you could vote in Kuwait was to be male and have a male relative there before 1920. And alcohol is okay there. No rivers or lakes or railroads: just desert. He says the Kuwaitis suck, they're the greediest people in the Gulf region!

Just what I want to hear while I wait to die for them. Just kidding, God! I'm not ready.

I guess you're not going to send a picture, my brother wrote Lynn, *but thanks a lot for the Christmas box. . . . I'm out here at night in the desert smelling of Elite and nuts. I have never read Stephen King. Is he a favorite of yours? We have a lot to learn about each other, don't we?*

You mentioned Mr. Raleigh in your letter so I guess he's still playing up at Linger. Since you don't go to B.H.S., you must run into him at your father's place.

You know the song "Linger" that Mr. Raleigh wrote and everyone likes to sing? It was really written to Joan, the cat, did you ever hear that? I think its real name is even "Joan's Song."

One Saturday afternoon when we were setting up for dinner, she came sneaking into The Grill with this yellow parakeet in her mouth, dead. It belonged to old Mrs. Leogrande from next door. Mr. Raleigh was fooling around at the piano, trying to write one of his songs. No one could get Joan out from under The Market Basket. So Mr. Raleigh said let her stay there since she'll be in for it soon enough. He called out, "Have fun while it lasts, Joan."

And he starts to sing. You know how it goes, I think. "What won't last won't go fast, Not here . . ." et cetera.

Anyhow, tell Mr. Raleigh I send greetings from the garden spot of the Middle East. Tell him I remember the day he wrote "Joan's Song," okay? You should listen to it sometime thinking of your killer cat devouring the bird except for a few yellow feathers. Your Desert Shield dude needs a photo. Enclosing one of me and my boys.

By that time, my brother was signing his letters to her *Love.*

That Christmas Day while he was getting ready to move deeper into the desert, we were heading into New York City for our annual outing with Uncle Chadwick.

I didn't look forward to these outings because we had to listen to Uncle Chad boast of his million-dollar deals, all accomplished because he had "the smarts." I missed my brother, who could always bring him down with a new lawyer joke (Bobby'd collect them for this occasion), like Uncle Chad, why did the elephant in the forest stop to eat a huge pile of lion dung? . . . You give up? Because he'd just swallowed a lawyer, and he wanted to get the bad taste out of his mouth.

Everyone in the family had the idea that just because I wanted to be a lawyer, I wanted to be like Uncle Chad, but I'd gotten my ambition from watching *L.A. Law*, not from watching my uncle spill Chivas Regal on his Ralph Lauren jacket as he pounded a table to make the point he was the best corporate troubleshooter in the whole U.S. of A.!

I think he used to impress Bobby way back; then Bobby grew out of it.

We were always treated by him to the annual Christmas Show at Radio City Music Hall, then early dinner somewhere.

I think of how my brother used to slump down in his seat and complain that he couldn't stand to hear *The Nutcracker* one more time, and that The Rockettes dancing across the stage in unison, in their red-and-green tutus, made him want to barf. But that was just Bobby's act. He had long ago assigned himself the role of

Grouch on Family Outings.

I think it was a way of sticking by our dad, too, since Uncle Chad was always out to prove to Mom and us boys that he was the better Peel. *We'd* landed the runt of the litter.

We were in a Chinese restaurant, after, and Uncle Chad was ordering for us, as if egg foo yung, pork lo mein, and chicken delight were must-try dishes we would never have had the sophistication to think of on our own.

And the pu-pu platter came first, aflame and bearing little paper parasols stuck into steamed dumplings.

He'd eat with chopsticks and chide us for not eating with them. After a few drinks, there'd be noodles next to the scotch stains on his jacket, duck sauce on his silk tie.

"So Bobby's really over there," he said.

"He wanted to be in the Army," my father said, sighing.

"You know, this was where I had lunch with Bobby some two or three years ago."

"When he came in to see Guns N' Roses that time?"

"One of those groups. That's when I told him

how to fix Mañana so Linger wouldn't have any competition."

We just looked at him. What did Bobby have to do with Mañana?

Mañana had been this little yellow shack, serving chicken and beef dishes with rice, and big pitchers of wine called sangría.

The only foreign food in Berryville, until this place opened, was Italian. We all wondered if a Mexican café could make it.

My father told my uncle, "Dunlinger lost a few dinners that summer, nothing serious."

"He was worried, though," my mother said. "When they set up that pretty little garden with the twinkling lights, he was worried."

"You see, this place had some competition once, too, right across the street," said Uncle Chad. "I told Bobby how this place took care of *their* competition. A little rumor got spread that the newly opened China Kite ought to be called China Cat, since they were serving dead stray cats from Times Square. . . . A few cat corpses, skinned, were found in their garbage pail."

There was a powerful silence for a second or two.

Then my mother said, "Mañana Meow."

That was the name that had been painted all over Berryville that summer, the same time there'd been the rumor about the stray cats the place got from the fields near the Canal.

"Is that what Bobby renamed it?" Uncle Chad chuckled.

"Bobby never —" my dad started to say.

My uncle snorted. "I told Bobby: People will believe *anything* about an ethnic place; just get the rumor going. Koreans eat cats for a fact, and I bet they do down Meh-hee-coh way, too. . . . Did it work?"

My father was shaking his head as though he couldn't believe it.

"Mr. Dunlinger felt awful about that rumor," said my mother.

"Bull merde, Wanda. Your Mr. Dunlinger probably gave Bobby a bonus!"

"This is the first I even heard about it," my father said. "Bobby never mentioned anything about Mañana."

"You were the last to know when he joined the Army, too, Charlie. I was the one who told him to get on the horn immediately and call you."

"He knew I wished he'd finish high school first."

"A kid's got to do what he's got to do," said Uncle Chad, who'd had two wives but no kids.

"Look where it got him," my mother said. "He's sitting in some desert in Saudi Arabia."

"We aren't going to war, Wanda," said Uncle Chad, "and that boy is having the experience of a lifetime. Nothing that exciting will ever happen to Bobby again!"

On the way back to Pennsylvania, I sat in the back listening to R.E.M. through headphones. I kept thinking about Mañana down by the Canal, everyone saying the mosquitoes would come up from the water nights and drive any customers crazy . . . or maybe it was Mr. Dunlinger who said that.

I remember once going by after a movie and my mother said, "Look!"

There were these colored lights, and a fellow in a big sombrero was playing guitar. Couples were dancing out on the stones, under the stars.

I remember my mother saying, "I never saw that in Berryville before!" And I remember seeing a kid I figured was about my own age in a red shirt and dark pants playing castanets. He had a cigarette dangling from his lips. He looked like a boy trying to look like a man; his face was too young to carry it off. Later I wondered if he was that Carlos Elizondo the papers wrote so much about.

Late that Christmas night we stopped for coffee and cake at this new place that had just opened when you crossed from New Jersey to Pennsylvania.

My mother and father loved going into new restaurants, comparing them with Linger.

My father finally brought up Mañana.

"Dunlinger *was* bothered by that place, wasn't he?"

"Charlie, Mr. D. felt sick about those rumors. Bobby too! You know Bobby has no hatred in him. None. He didn't have then and he doesn't have now!"

"I'm not talking about hatred," said my dad.

"Bobby thought it was funny, I think." I put in my two cents, even though I couldn't remember what Bobby'd thought about it at the time. "People were going by that place in their cars calling out the windows: 'Meow! Meow! Meow!'"

"Bobby would know it wasn't funny," Dad said. "And you know it wasn't funny, Gary. That was the beginning of the end for Mañana, Mr. Elizondo, *and* his boy, Carlos!"

My mother said, "Well, don't blame Bobby! You just said yourself he had no hatred in him."

"You said that, Wanda. *I* said I wasn't talking about hatred."

"What *are* you talking about then?"

"Bobby liked to pretend nobody and nothing ever impressed him, but Mr. D. *did*! You know how Bobby fought him. He never fought anyone that way but Mr. D.!"

"That's being impressed by somebody? Fighting him tooth and nail?"

My father shook his head. "That's caring."

"That's news to me," my mother said.

"We're his parents, his family," my father said. "He loves us somewhere inside him, but he could be indifferent to us, too. To most people. . . . But name me the one person Bobby wasn't *ever* indifferent to. Who was that?"

Nobody had to say who and nobody did.

10

We keep moving, columns of hummers wind-
ing across the sand, our bedrolls and tents tied
down. It's clammy cold.

Movie Star, Sugar, and me are the youngest
soldiers in the outfit. A lot of the others are
mothers and fathers, reservists who never figured they'd get called up for active duty, much
less for this war in the desert! Who did?

But we have left the women behind now.
They join a Marine Maintenance Unit, repair-
ing our M1 tanks, Bradleys etc., the first time
an Army unit has been attached to another
branch of the armed forces in combat. Marines
have put a limit on how far forward females
will go.

We are expecting war now, expecting the Iraqis to head straight our way, and we're issued our antitank weapons and keep our chemical suits and masks close.

Last night Movie Star said he wanted to have a lot of kids, but Sugar said not him. He said he wasn't going to do to any kid what was done to him, and he said, "I don't mean I ever got beat up or that stuff, my old man never got near enough to touch me. He'd never even look me in the eye. . . ." And he imitated him, got us laughing, as he does a lot!

Then Sugar asked us did we want to know about these wonderful people whose country we are saving called the Sabahs? I knew something was coming, because he is sort of a sardonic guy, and he goes, "Beautiful Kuwait is ruled by a noble merchant family called Sabah," in this musical tone. . . . His father knew one of the Sabahs very well, played golf with him a lot. This guy only wore a bathrobe one time. Later he would throw it out, a big, heavy, terry-cloth robe, just toss one away after every bath, or shower, or swim, and it wouldn't be laundered, just thrown away. He said everyone in the whole family had a Mercedes, even the daughters who didn't drive, each one had her own convertible that servants drove them in.

Sugar said they're all like that: rich, smug, spoiled rotten. The emir is probably off in London gambling while we fight his war, Sugar said. And this Kuwait is only the size of New Jersey; 90 percent is sand!

Movie Star keeps telling him to "cork it." He says he's heard enough crap about Kuwait. He's edgy anyway.

Movie Star says he has the feeling he's not going to get out of this alive, and Sugar says he has it, too, and it comes and goes. He says it's only natural, probably everyone has it at one point or another.

The trouble with me is it takes a long time for things to sink in. I'm like Dad that way. I'd say Why do you let Dunlinger talk to you like you're shit? Dad'd say Is he talking to me that way, Bobby? I hear him but I'm not sure he means any disrespect.

So I hear the hummers, and the planes, and the winds whipping sand into my face, and I think I'm hearing war but I'm not sure I hear "Taps."

I wonder if Lynn asked Mr. Raleigh about "Joan's Song."

She was never there late at night when everyone in the place would sing it. How did it go now, can I remember?

What won't last won't go fast,
Not here.
What is bad won't feel sad
In here.
So linger awhile, let's see that smile,
Secrets are mysteries still.
You'll have your way, you will.

Time is slow, do not go
From here,
And the scheme is a dream
In here.

So linger, so stay, it's always today,
Secrets are mysteries still.
You'll have your way, you will.

No one points a finger
When you are in Linger,

Not here,
Not in here,
Never here. . . .

Mr. Raleigh said since Barry Manilow wrote "Mandy" to his dog, he could write a song for Joan.

11

Have you been getting my letters regularly? my brother wrote. *I am writing once or twice a week, Lynn. So far I have the first one you wrote, the post-card, and the one inside your Christmas box, not that I'm not thanking you for writing me when you can get around to it because I am.*

I gulped when I saw what Mr. Raleigh'd copied out on his chalkboard.

At the bottom it said it was from a speech made by Senator Edward M. Kennedy, of Massachusetts, to members of the 102nd Congress, on the question of whether to let President Bush send out troops into war.

The administration refuses to release casu-alty estimates, but the 45,000 body bags the

Pentagon has sent to the region are all the
evidence we need of the high price in lives
and blood we will have to spare. . . . In other
words we're talking about the likelihood of at
least 3,000 American casualties a week, with
700 dead, for as long as the war goes on.

Mr. Raleigh had a basket on his desk filled with
new buttons: a big bloody thumb pointed down,
across it the same words he had hung on his bulletin board: All for Oil.

Only a few took one on the way out, after the
bell.

When I went by, he said, "Gary? Wait up."

He came hopping around the corner of his
desk, smiling at me. "How's Bobby doing?"

"Okay." Didn't he know Lynn was writing
Bobby?

"This button isn't against Bobby, you know.
It's *for* him, in the long run."

"I know." I wasn't sure I did.

"I hope you do. Maybe Bobby will get back to
writing."

"Not if they go to war."

"No. . . . Tell Bobby I'm surprised he remembered I used to call 'Linger' 'Joan's Song.'"

"I remember it, too. What'd he do, write you or something?"

"He wrote Mr. Dunlinger's daughter."

(Like he didn't know her name? Pass the barf bucket—I'm going to need it.)

He said, "Lynn had never heard how Joan inspired me to write that."

"Oh, yeah?"

He had this crooked grin on his face. He stuck his hand in his trouser pocket and rattled his change. "Say hi to Bobby for me, all right?"

"I'm not going to get my book report in by Friday, Mr. Raleigh," I said. "I've been watching CNN too much."

I thought it was worth a try, seeing if Bobby's being over in the Persian Gulf might buy me more time.

He kept grinning down at me. Said, "Then you get an F, Gary."

I sighed. "I'll get it in on time," I said.

"What book are you reading?"

"*The Sheltering Sky*."

"Come on, Gary. You're reading a novel from the forties set in Morocco? Just when the movie starts Thursday at Cinema One? No wonder you want extra time—time to see the movie so you don't have to read anything, right? What's your problem with reading? You know how much lawyers have to read?"

"Okay, okay," I said. "When I'm a lawyer, at least I'll get paid to read."

"Who's going to take the bar exam for you, Gary? . . . Now here, here's a book for you." He turned to get it from his desk. "Ever read *Coward* by Tom Tiede?"

He handed it to me. "It's not recent," he said.

On the front it said, *The story of a young draftee who refuses to fight in a war he cannot believe in.*

"I just finished a Stephen King," I said. "I'll do a report on that."

"Take this anyway," he said. "I don't mind you kids reading books made into movies, and thrillers, but it wouldn't hurt you to escape into a little reality now and then, too."

"Vietnam is reality?" I said, because I'd turned to the flap and seen *shipped to Vietnam*.

"There's going to be a lot of little Vietnams," he said, "and I'm afraid you kids are going to find them very real, unless you get more interested in what's going on."

"I'm interested," I said. "I did a paper on

those babies the Iraqis let die on the hospital floor, remember?"

"I'm trying to forget that paper."

"Because it gave a reason for us getting involved there?" He'd given me a D minus.

"Because it was copied almost word for word from a newspaper—a., and b., it was unsubstantiated, maudlin, and manipulative."

"What about FEEL FOR OTHER PEOPLE?"

He said, "Gary, every war has these reports of babies being pulled from their mothers' arms, or stuck with bayonets or left to starve, or some damn thing. That's manipulation. Women and children on both sides suffer during a war. But I want your attention focused on the issues, not the histrionics."

"You want all for oil," I said.

"Or find something that says it isn't. You could argue that Hussein is developing nuclear power. He probably is. You could argue for Israel. Or you could argue that if we don't defang Iraq and liberate Kuwait, we're going to be in for a much bigger war someday. Get me *thinking*, not crying in my beer over dying babies."

That weekend I went to see *The Sheltering Sky*

anyway. Berryville, on a Saturday night in January, has two offerings: the movie, or bowling at Knock 'Em Down.

Linger was closed two weeks for painting and repair, and Mom and Dad had gone to Sarasota, Florida, where her folks were.

The Dunlingers were taking off the next day for St. Bart's.

I figured Lynn was back at Faith Academy.

Some guys and I loaded up on popcorn, Coke, giant-sized Butterfingers, and boxes of little Milky Ways, planning on having our dinner in Cinema One.

We liked to sit practically in the front row and we were heading down there when Fred Schwartz said, "Mr. Raleigh's in the back row, d'you see him?"

"Mr. Give-Peace-a-Chance," Ollie Burns said.

"Give carrots a chance," Dave Leonard said.

"All we are say-ing," we all sang, "is give peas a chance."

I glanced over my shoulder and saw him sitting back there. I gave him a little salute and he winked back.

It was a boring movie set in the desert, and it made me miss Bobby, remembering he wrote us the desert sand got into everything. . . . At one point Ollie Burns came back from the bathroom and said, "I just saw your sweetheart, Lynn Dunlinger, sneak in with Gloria Yee and sit down by Mr. Raleigh."

"*My* sweetheart!" I said. (Don't I wish.)

"Shhhut up!" Dave Leonard whispered. He didn't care what was up there on the big screen, he went and lived there.

Some people behind us said, "Shhhhhhh!"

I couldn't resist whispering, "Lynn Dunlinger is back in school, so it wasn't her."

"It was *her*!" Ollie Burns said.

"Shhhhhhh!" people behind us hissed.

I turned around and looked up at the back row.

Gloria Yee was there, all right, but Lynn wasn't.

Neither was Mr. Raleigh. Not anymore.

12

—*from the journal of Private Robert Peel*
Saudi Arabia

Sugar says, "You never say her name. Like what's her name, Roberto?"

"Lynn Dunlinger. Okay? Lynn."

I don't think I ever said her name to her face. I always went out of my way not to have to speak to her.

Sugar says he has no girl and admits he is a virgin. He says he was never in one place long enough to date, thanks to his father, who dragged him with him from one country to another. He wouldn't even send him to prep school, even though he had bucks. He'd leave Sugar alone nights in strange lands to be with women. Sugar joined up as soon as he was old enough, to get away from him. Never thought

67

there'd be a war. The familiar refrain over here.

I tell him about my first time, with Cheryl Sledd. What I hated most was driving home after when she said it was too fast for her to enjoy and I didn't give her time to get in the mood. I said, "Is this a report card, Teacher?"

"If it is, you get F plus," she said. "The plus is because I didn't have to use my own condom."

Second time was Betty Chayka. Chike. I held back and it was good for her I think because we dated for a few months. She'd say she wanted to see the green light in my car, nights we'd do it.

Movie Star says when a Mexican girl is fifteen, she has a party called a *quinceanera*; she wears a frilly dress and dances her first dance with her father. His sister is having hers this week, and we all signed a card he made for her: Congratulations, Gina!

13

I hear you're writing Lynn Dunlinger, I wrote my brother. *I hope you're not falling for her, since you'd have to get in line. Only kidding! I know you better.*

Joan, the cat, wore a yellow ribbon, and there was one tied to every tree, lamppost, railing, and fence on Linger property.

Mr. Dunlinger handed me three large ones, already tied, with two wires attached behind the bows, ready for hanging.

"These are to go up on the outside porch of Lingering Shadows," he told me.

"Yes, Sir."

"You don't have to sir me, Gary. But I admit I like that you do. Bobby never did."

"No, Sir. He's not the type."

"When you write him, you tell him we miss him around here, will you do that?"

"Yes, sir."

"Oh, I know he's writing my daughter and she could tell him, but I don't think Lynn will remember to, and I don't think she's a very frequent correspondent."

"I'll remember to tell him."

"I want you to check the smoke alarm in Lingering Shadows, and the burglar alarm, too. Lynn will be staying there weekends. Her mother and I agree that she should have a place of her own. And I think she'll visit us more often this way. I used to never be able to get her away from Faith Academy. Now she's coming home nearly every weekend."

I knew that. I'd see them together walking out back, or she'd sit in the bar and watch him play. Nothing obvious. But I knew.

Mr. Dunlinger made the same leap from Lynn to Jules Raleigh, and I flinched as he said, "I'm assigning you a spy mission, too, where Jules is concerned. Who else would give you permission to spy on your teacher? . . . I want you to keep an eye on him."

I was dumbstruck, a state of being which I think Mr. Dunlinger preferred from his help.

He said, "I've told him I want an upbeat patriotic song to start every set, and I want them blended into the mood music as well."

"Did he agree?"

"He works for me. There's no disagree to it if he wants his paycheck. But he wrinkled up his face, and it wouldn't surprise me if he'd forget when I'm not around. . . . I want you to jog his memory."

"Yes, Sir." That was all.

"And everyone is to wear a yellow ribbon and a flag."

"Did you tell Mr. Raleigh that?"

"I told him." Mr. Dunlinger dug down into his pocket, felt around, and then took out a tiny lapel flag and an envelope. He said, "Give Mr. Raleigh this flag. He claimed he could find a ribbon but not a flag."

"He's not going to like it," I said. "You know how he feels about us being over there."

"Everybody in this county knows how he feels. I could fire him tomorrow and nobody'd blink an eye."

"I'll give him this," I said.

"Linger is like a little country, Gary. We have

our customs and our ways and our beliefs. You can visit us without subscribing to any of it . . . but if you're a Lingerite, you do what the rest do."

It was right on the dot of six, and Mr. Raleigh began to play in The Regency Room. Both Mr. Dunlinger and I paused to listen.

I'd never heard "America the Beautiful" played on the violin.

Mr. Dunlinger looked pleased.

Then he handed me the envelope.

"Lynn asked me to give this to you."

Just beyond The Grill, there was a little hallway where I paused and ripped open the envelope.

There was a note and two photographs.

The note said, *Dear Gary, I thought you and your folks would like to have these. . . . Very best, L.*

One was a group picture. Bobby was standing between two other guys, a good-looking dark-haired fellow and a tall blond. The three of them were in boots and camouflage uniforms, and Bobby was the only one with a big smile.

He'd written across the top *Augustin "Movie Star" Sanchez, Bobby (Roberto) Peel, and Donald*

"Sugar" Sweet send greetings from The Gulf. December 1990.

The other photo was just Bobby.

He had on a white T-shirt with two bayonets crossed over the letters "U.S." in red, white and blue, and beneath that in enormous brown letters

ARMY

He had on the usual camouflage pants, and boots, but on his head he was wearing one of those things that look like dish towels. He was pounding his chest, big grin on his face.

On this one he'd written *Luv, Bobby*.

About a week ago we'd gotten the same ones in a letter from him, only the one of him alone said *Your hero!* On the back it said, *I traded hats with a dude on a camel. This kind of headgear's called a kaffiyeh.*

I suppose I should have been glad she didn't treasure Bobby's photos, but I hated it. All I could think of was him over there in a strange land he could easily die in, writing Lynn Dunlinger, who didn't even want a picture of him.

It wasn't her fault—I knew that, too.

On my way up to Lingering Shadows, I tore them into tiny pieces and tossed them in a trash bin. I didn't want my brother ever to know.

14

Sugar makes up new words to an old song from *South Pacific*.

> *We got sunlight, we got sand,*
> *We got moonlight, we got stars,*
> *We got mail from home for kicks,*
> *And we're up to here in dicks,*
> *We got Movie Star and Bobby,*
> *And we never get afraid,*
> *But what can't we get?*
> *We can't get laid!*

Later we turn on Desert Shield Radio, and a Phil Collins song is interrupted: "We *repeat*: Congress gave President Bush authority to drive Iraqi troops from Kuwait."

Outside the tent some guys are cheering.

15

There was a snowstorm and it was bitter cold, so Mom picked me up after school. She'd come from Linger, where she was working now instead of at home, because she said it felt so good to be there.

"You feel safe there," she told me.

"*You* feel safe there. I feel like a gofer there." But I was grumbling pointlessly, because I liked it there too. When anything big happened, people gravitated toward the place, whether it was a World Series win, a scandal, or the threat of war.

Mom had on fur earmuffs, and I hoped they'd keep out the noise ahead of us, on the sidewalk in front of The Berryville Trust.

"Mr. D. found a tape of patriotic music, and it plays through the system all day. Sometimes I wipe the tears away," she said.

Then we saw the signs that went with the shouts.

NO BODIES FOR BARRELS!
SANCTIONS . . . NOT SLAUGHTER!
HOW DID ALL *OUR* OIL GET UNDER
THEIR SAND?
ALL FOR OIL

There was the big ex-Marine from Scott Contractors, carrying a placard that said, MESS WITH THE BEST, DIE WITH THE REST, but he was the only one there with that sentiment.

I knew most of the people. They were what Mr. D. called "the NOW crowd," mostly women. You'd see them out demonstrating for abortion, various environmental concerns, AIDS support . . . or they'd be against some judge who was nominated for the Supreme Court, or the nuclear plant they wanted to build across the line in New Jersey, or hunting in The Pine Barrens, or gun ownership.

There was a local librarian; a woman who ran an amateur theater company; Osborne de la Marin the Fourth and his mother; my dentist's wife; Mrs. Wheat pushing her quadriplegic Vietnam War veteran son; Pauline Wheat, the daughter; Sloan Scott, who I'd always had my eye on; and of course, *he* was there.

Mom said, "Jules is a fool! If I never knew it before, I know it now."

"What are you doing?"

"Pulling over."

"Mom, don't start."

"I didn't. *They* did!"

She was parked before I knew it, and out of the car before I could finish asking her what she was planning to do. I got out, too, my hands stuffed in my jacket pockets, hanging back, not wanting the scene.

"For your information, my boy is over there!"

"Then God help him!" said Leonard Wheat.

My mother calmed down a little. She wasn't about to argue with a man who'd lost the use of his arms and legs in Vietnam. I heard her telling him what was wrong with his war was that people at home weren't supportive. And I heard him tell her war was wrong whether or *not* the people supported it.

Then Mrs. Wheat got in on the act, and my dentist's wife, so I stayed out of it, leaned against the car, and watched my breath freeze-frame my sighs.

Betty Chayka came down Osborne Street (named for the ancestors of Osborne de la Marin the Fourth) on her way to work at Berryville Video Store.

"Good for your mother!" she said.

Even in a down coat Chike was a sexpot. She just was. Something about her—I knew what Bobby meant when he said there were a lot of girls more beautiful, but not a one in Berryville with a better game.

I said, "Well, it'll make her feel better, maybe."

Chike laughed and bumped against me. "What would make *you* feel better?" She smelled like a women's magazine.

"You would," I said.

"You're getting to look more like Bobby every day."

"Yeah, but I'm not Bobby."

She hooted at that and said, "You don't have to tell *me* that! I know you're not Bobby."

Somehow she was insulting me, but I didn't care. She did everything with a smile.

She said, "When you write him? Tell him I still like green light."

"Oh yeah?" I said. "I don't like any light at all."

"Amateurs don't." She smiled and touched a gloved finger to my chin. "And tell Bobby I got yellow ribbons all over my old oak tree for him, okay?"

I could see Mom down the way surrounded by the group of protesters. I wondered if I should rescue her when I saw Mr. Raleigh take her by the arm and start back toward our car.

Mom was crying, and Mr. Raleigh said, "Better get her home, Gary."

"*You* go home!" my mother shouted back at him. "Go home to Russia where you belong!"

I watched him stagger away on his built-up shoe. He always made me feel bad when I watched him walk.

"How'd Russia get into this, Mom?" I asked her when we got into the car.

She said, "He can go to hell!"

She'd never talked that way before, and when I looked across at her face, she didn't look like herself.

Much, much later, I tried to tell myself that: She wasn't herself. She didn't do things like that.

16

Both Sugar and Movie Star write "To Be Opened in Case of My Death" letters. Sugar's is for his father. He says he's going to write him: Looks like I had to die to live. Movie Star writes two: to his family and then to Amy. I don't write one because it might bring it about.

But I think about one to Mr. D.

"They are coming up here and taking the food right out of our mouths," he said. "Taking our ideas, our jobs, our land, and the ones who're legal are taking our welfare. These are people who really mean mañana never comes if mañana means staying where they belong and making something out of their own land.

"What they lack," he said, "is national

pride. Do you see a flag of any kind hanging from that shack?"

I said, "They serve their own food, and they play their own music."

"Bobby," he said, "if I say the sky is blue, you point out the white clouds, and that's what's wrong with you. You don't like me to say wetback, but you never had to fight for a dream, work your ass off for one—give up college for one. When somebody older and smarter tells you something: LISTEN! Don't always look for a contrary sentiment.

"LISTEN, Bobby!" he said. "*Learn!* That's how you develop entrepreneurial skills. You don't learn them at your daddy's knee, or in school. You learn them from someone who's got what it takes. You take what he's got. You don't tell him he doesn't have it, and you don't tell him what's wrong with what he has. You listen and learn!"

"Okay," I said, "but . . ."

"Okay, *Mr. D.*," he said.

"Okay, Mr. D., but what can they do to us?"

"LISTEN AND LEARN, Bobby! They, be they from Mexico, the Dominican Republic,

Colombia—and these are the ones moving in on us—be they from Ecuador or El Salvador, on and on: They are *encroaching* upon us. Do you know what that word means?"

"Moving in," I said.

"Intruding is a better word," he said, "intruding upon someone's territory, rights, or time . . . or all three."

"Just like the Japs have zapped us," I said.

He said, "Mañana *we'll* be beholden to little greaseball men in sombreros who look like dirty thumbs with hats on!"

17

My night off. We ate at Linger, guests of Mr. D.

Mrs. D. was at Berryville Presbyterian Church fixing boxes for the troops, filling them with paperbacks, cans of Spam, M&M's, cigarettes, socks, long underwear, et cetera.

We ate in The Grill so we could watch TV and Dan Rather, who was Mr. D.'s favorite news commentator.

I could hear "The White Cliffs of Dover" coming from The Regency Room where Mr. Raleigh was entertaining some of the regulars who always turn out on Tuesdays for the corned beef and cabbage Linger features.

"What you tell me about Jules is very disturbing, Wanda," said Mr. D., "yet a man has a right to his opinions. But if he pulled any of that peace stuff up here, I'd deck him."

I was chomping on my corned beef, trying to

picture Mr. D. decking Jules Raleigh. I'd never seen him raise his hand to anyone, much less a cripple. He didn't even raise his voice.

"I wish he wasn't teaching kids," said my mother.

"We don't pay any attention to him," I said. I was trying to defend him in my own way, but I suppose I was making it worse.

"Even my own little girl thinks our troops shouldn't be over there, which makes me sad," said Mr. Dunlinger. "But she says she's not the only one at Faith Academy to feel that way, including some of the priests."

"That's hard to believe," said my father.

"We had those priests, the Berrigans, during Vietnam, remember?" Dunlinger said. "They ransacked the Selective Service office and burned all the 1-A classification records."

"This is no Vietnam," said my mother.

I remember in class Mr. Raleigh said the government had learned from Vietnam that all the killing people watched nightly on TV turned them against the war. He said if there's a war in the Gulf, the government will control the media. You'll see a lot of fireworks but you won't see people getting killed.

Mr. Dunlinger said to me, "At least you don't have to worry, Gary. This will be all ancient history by the time you're eighteen. You'll go right off to college."

One subject we carefully avoided around Mr. D. was Bobby. Okay if he brought it up, but we didn't. Among ourselves we also didn't bring up Mañana Meow now. All we cared about was Bobby getting back safely. Anything that had gone down before he was shipped to the Gulf was peanuts compared to what he was up against.

But ever since our dinner with Uncle Chad I kept trying to imagine what could have made Bobby use that cat thing against Mañana, what could have made him *care* that Linger was losing a little business, if it was?

Was my father right? Had Dunlinger had so much power over Bobby that he'd go to any length to impress him? . . . Was it because Bobby needed someone like Dunlinger to look up to, since our father was such a milksop?

After all, I'd had Bobby for a hero . . . until last Christmas dinner with Uncle Chad. Then I had my doubts about Bobby, for the first time.

And I kept remembering the kid in the red shirt smoking the cigarette, and though I only saw him that one time, it was in my head he'd been Carlos Elizondo.

"I had to help my father get this place underway—it was our dream. I never went to college," Mr. Dunlinger said as though that was any news to us. He said it often enough for me to know that the next words would be *And I don't think I turned out that bad*.

"Not everybody has your entrepreneurial skills," said my mother, who'd learned the last two words in the sentence from Mr. Dunlinger.

Himself said, "And I don't think *I* turned out that bad." He put his finger to his lips. Dan Rather had come on. We all began to give our attention to CBS, the TV competing with Mr. Raleigh's rendition of that Tchaikovsky concerto I knew as "Tonight We Love."

That started me thinking about Lynn Dunlinger and Mr. Raleigh. Not only had I kept what I knew secret, I'd even convinced Ollie Burns he'd been seeing things that night we went to *The Sheltering Sky*.

I kept thinking of her eyes when she said, "Don't tell," and of my promising her I wouldn't.

One weekend when the Dunlingers were still on vacation she'd spent her nights in The Grill watching him. He'd sung to her and sat with her on breaks. I kept looking from their faces to Mr. Yee's, wondering why he couldn't see what was going on between them. Maybe he could.

I was mulling that over as we sat there, and then Dave Leonard came out of the kitchen in his waiter's uniform and shouted, "We're at war!"

Mr. Dunlinger jumped to his feet and said we were nothing of the kind, but Dave insisted: "Watch CNN!"

The bartender switched the channel and we saw a picture of the reporter, Bernard Shaw, superimposed over a map of Iraq.

"This is extraordinary," he was saying. "The lights are still on. All the streetlights in downtown Baghdad are still on. But as you look, you see trails of flashes of light going up into the air, obviously antiaircraft fire. We're getting starbursts. . . ."

We all sat there in shock listening, and when a man from the Pentagon came on to say the President would be going on television later, Mr. Dunlinger got to his feet. "I'm going downtown to get my Natalia," he said. "We *are* at war."

The violin was silent. So was everything but the television.

18

"You have to outsmart these little varmints," Mr. Dunlinger said. "Half of them can be picked up for being undocumented aliens. There's a fine, you know, for employing undocumented aliens. That's what half of them are who're up here taking jobs away from good Americans," he said.

He said, "Bobby, nobody ever handed me anything! I came up the hard way. I earned everything I have by the sweat of my brow, working alongside my father."

"But you're smart, too, Mr. D."

"You bet your behind I'm smart! It's not *just* hard work *ever*, Bobby."

I remember I said, "Or my dad would have gone farther."

He looked away from me.

He murmured, "He does what he does well enough."

"I don't aspire to be like him," I said.

Mr. D. laughed hard at that. He said, "I never imagined you did *aspire* to be like him." He said, "*Aspire* is a beautiful word, Bobby, if you've got the imagination and the guts to go with it."

He said, "It's not that I'm not amused by the China Cat idea. It's just that these far-fetched, fly-by-night schemes are usually pipe dreams."

He put his big hand on my head and mussed up my hair, in that old good-dog-good style.

"But I appreciate it, Bobby. Your heart's in the right place."

I was thinking both things ought to do it. Mañana Meow plus the undocumented aliens. They had to have a few down there, didn't they? If only out of sight, in the kitchen. It'd cost them, plus it'd make them even more un-popular: aliens taking our jobs!

19

"God bless America," Mrs. Dunlinger was singing. She was in The Regency Room that night in late January. In The Grill, Desert Storm was on CNN. No one wanted to watch any other channel.

Any family with a serviceperson who was assigned to the Gulf was entitled to a two-for-one dinner. One couple whose daughter was over there came from Philadelphia for filet mignon with mashed. Mr. Dunlinger had them sign her name on the honor roll in the hall, and he sent them two glasses of complimentary wine.

The walls were festooned with red, white, and blue crepe paper; the ceiling with yellow ribbons; and on every table by the salt and pepper, there was a little stand with a cotton American flag stuck in it.

"Did you put Bobby's name on the honor

roll?" Mr. Dunlinger asked me.

"No, Sir."

"Well, do it! When this war is won, we're going to have one bang-up celebration here, and everyone on that honor roll is going to be my guest!"

He'd taken out ads in the county newspapers, and he had a commercial on WTGH: LINGER THANKS OUR BRAVE ARMED FORCES!

While I was writing Bobby's name in, Mr. Raleigh came by to ask me if I'd speak to the substitute piano player that weekend about Mr. D.'s idea to have patriotic songs in every set.

"Where are you going?" I asked him.

"I'm going to Vermont to visit my son," he said. "I might do some tobogganing, too. What do you hear from Bobby?"

"He says they travel like a train, fifty-eight sand-colored tanks on the move."

"At least he's inside."

"When he's not in the turret. He wrote one time 'How do you get wet riding in a tank? You ride in the turret and the rain runs down your flak jacket, soaks your pants, your boots—try to sleep after that,' he wrote."

Mr. Raleigh hobbled away, calling over his shoulder, "Tell Bobby I'm praying for him."

Dad was working late because the war was bringing more people to Linger. Usually everyone was gone by nine thirty or ten on a weeknight, but now they were staying.

I decided to go home and keep Mom company. I also wanted to watch CNN. I'd never seen a war on TV. I wasn't even born for Vietnam. The only wars I'd ever watched were in the movies.

We sat in the living room for a while, viewing video-game-style bombs explode while reporters stood in front of planes and American flags talking about "sorties" and "Scuds" and "Patriot missiles."

"I can't watch anymore," Mom finally said.

"Why don't we watch a tape?"

"You go to bed—it's midnight. I'll watch a tape."

"What have you got?"

"I taped the Sally Jessy Raphael show this morning. I had to go up to Linger to meet the decorator who's doing Lingering Shadows over.

I'll sew the curtains."

She'd started smoking again ever since the war began.

She was only going to smoke one Camel a day, outdoors.

I watched her light up. "Shall I get you an ashtray?" I said sarcastically.

She knew how to deal with me. "I hate it that he's over there," she said.

"Yeah, well . . . What's Sally Jessy got on?"

"I find it so very hard to believe Bobby spread that cat rumor. Your father won't even discuss it."

"I don't want to either."

"It's no way to remember your brother."

"I don't remember him that way," I said.

"How do you remember him?"

"I remember him calling us the cool, cool Peel brothers and chasing Chike, stuff like that. And our Sunday walks. What *is* this?"

"Remember how protective he was?"

"What *is* this? He's not dead."

"No, but remember how he'd tell Daddy not to let Dunlinger use that tone of voice on him? And if Daddy didn't want to go with me to a movie, Bobby'd go with me, always. I think he joined the Army because he wanted you to get all the college money. He always said you were the brain."

I was sliding the tape into the VCR, trying not to get the guilts at the thought of the college money. Every time Dad didn't want to replace something on its last legs, he'd say, "Gary's too close to college now."

Mom said, "Bobby wouldn't hurt a fly, Gary. That boy, that Carlos, the newspapers said he was high-strung or something. What did they say he was?"

"They said he'd had emotional problems even before he was turned in. At least Bobby didn't turn him in."

"And Bobby didn't realize what Mañana Meow would do to their business. Bobby was just a kid back then!"

"Dunlinger probably egged him on. He couldn't stand the idea of having their kind for competition. . . . But let's not sweat it, Mom." I didn't like to think about it.

Mom said, "We don't say *sweat* in this house, we say perspiration. And we don't say *their kind* anywhere!"

"Don't perspire over it. I was being sarcastic,

talking like Mr. D."

"I never, ever heard Mr. D. talk like that."

"Bobby heard him. He told me he did."

"Mr. D. is one of the finest human beings I know."

"Don't get carried away, Mom."

"I just hope Mr. D. and Bobby do make up, now that Bobby and Lynn are getting together."

I didn't even want to answer that. The tape was playing. I said, "Stop worrying, Mom. It'll be okay!"

Sally Jessy's show was beauty makeovers for spouses of Persian Gulf warriors.

20

Iraqi deserters descend on us. They're hungry and scared. They wolf down the MREs, the only ones ravenous enough to be thankful for them.

A few guys want souvenirs from them for the food: a ring, a chain, a religious medal, though it's against regulations to loot.

Movie Star says he goes along with the regulations. His ancestors had this superstition some in his family swear is true. If you steal from someone, you steal their bad luck, too.

Do I have what would be left of Carlos Elizondo's bad luck now?

All that summer I waited for Dunlinger to say

something to me, to acknowledge it was no pipe dream. I'd pulled it off single-handed, with only mob psychology for help and an eventual assist from the police investigating the "anonymous" phone tip about illegals.

Dunlinger was in high spirits when Mañana turned into Mañana Meow. He never referred to it, though; he shrugged off the employees' jokes about it. Only once did I hear him laugh and say we'd better keep Joan in, if the gossip was true.

I remember the night Mr. Yee told him Mr. Elizondo's son and nephew were arrested as illegal employees. While Mr. Elizondo and his brother had papers, his wife and most of his children were still in Mexico. The son and his cousin had sneaked into the country to help at Mañana.

Mr. Dunlinger didn't say anything, and a week or so later, when Mr. Yee said something terrible had happened to Carlos Elizondo, Mr. Dunlinger said, "*Who?*"

"The son who was arrested for being an illegal."

"Did they send him back to where he came from?"

"He hung himself, Mr. D."

He caught me by the arm that night, out in back of Linger, as I was leaving.

He almost whispered what he said; it took me a few seconds to realize no, he was *hissing*. That was the sound when he said didn't I know the difference between idle chitchat and a deliberate plan of action? Did I *seriously* think he would have let me do such a thing if he had known my intentions? Well? Well? Did I? *Did* I?

I said, "You never tried to stop me."

"When did I know you were a maniac? After it was a *fait accompli*!"

"You had to know it was me, Mr. D. I told you about the China Cat."

"You talk to me when I'm busy. You think I remember every little word from your mouth?"

It must have been the day of the funeral when Mr. Elizondo showed up in Linger's kitchen. He was in a black suit, carrying a hat that looked too hot to wear on a late-summer afternoon.

"I just want to see what kind of a face someone like you has," he said to Mr. Dunlinger.

I was standing right beside them. I thought maybe he had a knife. His voice was so eerily soft, his brow beaded with sweat. He was breathing hard.

I should have said that it was me he should talk to, not Dunlinger, but all I managed to say to him was "Don't hurt him."

Then he turned and looked at me and shook his head.

"Hurt him?" he said. "I could never do to him what he has done to himself. He has become what he is, and now he lives with it."

As soon as Mr. Elizondo left, Mr. Dunlinger said to me, "Let's get out of here!"

He didn't want to talk in front of the cook and the one busboy who was in the back stacking plates.

"Just forget it happened," he told me out in the hall.

He was angry, and it made me hate myself and him.

I said, "Next time say it was me who did it. Don't protect me, okay? Don't do me any favors. Okay?"

"Don't *you* do *me* any more," he said. He

slammed out of there. He didn't come back until after dinner, when he had Mrs. Dunlinger with him. I never knew what he'd told her about it, if he'd told her anything or let her believe what most people at Linger thought: Some kids started the cat rumor. And the search for undocumented aliens was just routine, and a coincidence.

After I left work that night I never went back.

I never told anyone the truth.

I don't think he did, either.

Carlos Elizondo was twelve, *The Berryville Record* reported, but he always looked older. He was sensitive, they quoted his father; he got scared when the police took him in. He'd only been in this country a year.

Why Mañana? the paper questioned on its editorial page. A few miles east a Thai restaurant has *never* been investigated, and across the Canal neither have a Chinese and a Japanese, nor the Mexican one in Kingston. And what about the summer inns throughout the county that hire itinerant help? Why was this one the scapegoat?

Once I thought I would write a letter to Mr. Elizondo and tell him *I* was the one, and I was sorry. But who knew where he was, where they had gone after they cleared out of Berryville?

21

Thanks a lot for the photographs, Lynn, my brother wrote. *Where were they taken? I have never tobogganed, myself. Maybe after this is finished you can show me how. How about it?*

Thumbtacked next to Linger's Guest Suggestion Box one Sunday morning in February was a petition to get rid of Jules Raleigh.

It was signed by twenty regular customers. It said:

> How can we enjoy the patriotic songs he plays and sings when we know next day he'll be back on the street with the antiwar demonstrators? We do not feel it is in the spirit of Linger to harbor a flag burner.

"He never burned a flag," Lynn Dunlinger told her father. "That's just hyperbole."

She was home for the weekend, staying in Lingering Shadows even though things weren't finished. My mother was still working on the drapes; the new carpeting hadn't been installed either.

Mr. Dunlinger said, "Does your being here every other weekend mean you plan to take over the running of this place?"

They were standing in the hall, outside The Regency Room.

She said, "I just don't think you should fire Mr. Raleigh."

"I'm not going to. I'd have to boot you out, too, wouldn't I?"

I was trying to sweep up around them. We were expecting The Pennsylvania Realtors for lunch. Everyone was talking about what a good summer it was going to be for rentals and sales and tourist business.

Everyone was afraid to go to Europe, figuring the terrorists would be out in full force now that the war was raging. My father wouldn't even let my mother go down to Key West, Florida, to visit Uncle Paul as she did every year. Dad didn't want her in the air, or in any airport, although President Bush's wife had taken a commercial flight to Indianapolis to show air travel was safe.

"Mr. Dunlinger?" I said. "Shall I take the petition down?"

"No. Any customer who feels obliged to sign it is entitled. . . . What I want *you* to do, Gary, is get all those gifts for our servicemen down to the basement. We're going to wrap and box them this afternoon."

"Service*people*," said Lynn.

"Get all those gifts for our service*people* out of the way, you hear me, Gary?"

"Yes, Sir."

"Hi, Gary!"

"Hello, Lynn."

Where the Christmas tree and the toys for the Eloise kids were every December, Dunlinger had roped off an area and had a sign printed.

GIFTS FOR THE PERSIAN GULF HEROES
YOU BRING THEM HERE.
WE'LL WRAP AND MAIL THEM.

My mother and I were the we.

No one came to Linger, anymore, without something for the box, and those customers who hadn't known about it tossed in cash.

When Lynn offered to help me carry stuff down, her father said, "Let her wrap some for you, too, Gary. She turns gift wrapping into an art."

"I've got a lunch date, Daddy, or I would."

"Invite her here to have lunch on me."

"Maybe it's not a her, Daddy."

"You got a boyfriend I don't know about?" He laughed as though it was a big joke.

I could hear her coming down the stairs behind me.

"Be careful," I said. "The light isn't very bright."

"Your mother's making me the most beautiful drapes!"

"I heard."

She put the boxes on the counter with the others. There was a small mountain of them. I figured I could kiss most of my Saturday goodbye. But Dunlinger was paying me double time to do it, and that would give me money for my date that night with Sloan Scott.

Dave Leonard had a date, too. We were all going to see *The Silence of the Lambs*.

Lynn had on one of those real short skirts, a

red one, with a sweater as black as her hair. She seemed to be waiting for me. I could feel her behind me as I was separating the small packages from the large ones.

I turned around, and she said, "I don't know what to do about Bobby, Gary."

"What do you mean?"

"I can't keep writing to him."

"What do you mean?"

"He's getting a little more serious each letter."

I kept saying, "What do you mean?" even though I knew what she meant. It didn't take any brains to figure out how he could want something to be real that wasn't, stuck over there in the middle of a war.

"Gary, can I trust you?"

"Yes."

"I'm in love with Jules and I think he's in love with me."

"I figured as much. That night you met him at the movie, I told the guys they were seeing things, but I knew they weren't."

"I got off the bus to school and made Gloria go there with me. I knew he was there. He was furious with me for showing up like that, but I can't help myself sometimes."

I couldn't think of anything to say. I could smell her perfume.

"I know he's a teacher, and he's older, but he's not *my* teacher, and in July he'll only be six years older than I am."

"What are you going to do?" I asked her.

"He says we have to wait. He says when I'm eighteen if we still want to date each other, we have to tell Daddy."

"That's only five months."

"I moved into Lingering Shadows just so I can be near him. I can hear him play from up there. He won't even come up there now."

"Maybe you should just tell your father."

"What do you think my father would do, Gary?"

"I think he'll blow," I said.

"Exactly. But when I'm eighteen I can do what I want."

"Like what? Start dating him?"

"I want to marry him. I could marry him."

"Marry him?"

"You should see your face, Gary."

"What's the matter with it?" I knew. It was red. I could feel it. I was acting out what I felt:

that I was being burned, even when she'd never paid any attention to me. She meant something to me just the same. She meant a lot.

She was kind enough not to tell me what was the matter with my face. She went on with what she was saying. "He does love me, Gary. When someone loves you, you know. But Daddy is difficult. You know that. It doesn't help that Jules is opposed to the war, either."

"Can't he soft-pedal it a little?"

"I wouldn't have any respect for him if he did," she said, making me feel shitty for suggesting it.

She said, "Anyway, Daddy's not going to think anyone is good enough for me."

"I know."

"He already told me I could only *write* Bobby, that when Bobby comes home I can't date him."

"Did he say why?"

"He said it wasn't right for management to get involved with employees."

"Bobby would never want his old job back."

"I know that. It's just an excuse."

"Bobby will still be in the Army after the war."

"I *know*. I'm just trying to tell you Daddy's

impossible when it comes to me and boys." Then she corrected herself and said "Men."

"But your dad seems to like Mr. Raleigh okay, so maybe—"

She shook her head no.

She said, "He'll hate it. He's already made cracks about his leg keeping him from making more of himself. Daddy says why didn't he get a Ph.D? He says Jules doesn't accept his handicap as a challenge; he just gives in to it, or he wouldn't be teaching high school in Berryville."

"I thought he really liked Mr. Raleigh."

"He does. But Daddy's son-in-law has to be a combination of Jesus Christ, Donald Trump, and General Schwarzkopf, and he can't be seven years older than I am."

"Six, in July," I said masochistically.

"Right! . . . Jules is saving to go to graduate school, and I could go to the same college. I don't need Daddy's money, either. I'll work my way through."

"You could do that," I said.

"He's had a hard life, Gary. When the little boy was born that way, his wife said it was his fault, that he had defective genes! Can you imagine? She just walked out!"

I didn't have anything to say.

"Gary?"

"What?"

"His hands tremble when I touch him."

"Neat," I said. I felt like I'd been run over in traffic.

"He calls me Ling. Nobody's ever called me by a special name. Sometimes he calls me Lingerling."

I had to look away from her face.

"I've never been in love. I'm just so happy."

"Good. That's good."

"So could you handle the Bobby thing for me? Somehow?"

"You mean tell him?"

"You can't say who it is. Not to anyone, Gary."

"You mean write him and tell him you're in love with someone?"

"Don't you think so? Before he comes home and —"

"I don't know about that."

"Gary, I can't keep writing him and sending my picture and everything, or he'll feel I'm his girl."

"Yeah."

"If he doesn't already. How do I know that he doesn't already feel that?"

"Could we hold off and let me think about this?" I asked her.

"Yes. Do whatever is right."

"I don't think you should just stop writing him in the middle of a war."

"I know. I feel *awful*."

"So just write him," I said, "and let me think."

"All right, I will," she said. "And Gary?"

"Yeah?"

"Don't tell a soul about Jules."

"Okay."

"Promise me?"

"Yes," I said, hoping the damn stinging behind my eyes didn't develop into anything.

But she didn't hang around anyway.

She had a date.

22

—*from the journal of Private Robert Peel*
Iraq

We keep rolling. After tank plows make the breach lanes, they run right over Iraqi bunkers and trenches, plowing the men under.

Once, Sugar speaks up: Since *when* is it okay to bury men alive?

Lieutenant Kerin says what's the difference if you kill them that way or with hand grenades or bayonets? We're *here* to kill them!

Then we get the first taste of it, tanks in flames, sky coming apart with BOOMS like thousands of oil drums falling, exploding in the sand, BOOM! BOOM! BOOM!

Then guns, cannons, rocket launchers all going. Gunners use night-vision sights to locate T72's in the black smoke and dust.

Five A.M. Finally we sleep in shifts, hammocks strung inside the tank. I loop my canvas-pack harness around the Bradley seat to sleep, so I don't topple to the floor if we start up again. We keep the engines at idle to be ready to move out fast.

By seven we hear the medevac helicopters swarming through the sky to lift the wounded out of the mud.

Low overcast and cold rain, and outside everywhere dead bodies are strewn, and parts of bodies, and there is twisted steel, wreckage, looks like a junkyard as the fog lifts.

The radio is filled with reports of Iraqi soldiers surrendering by the thousands. Marine and Arab forces hitting hard at Iraq's 3rd Armored Division outside Kuwait. . . . War may be over!

Sugar sings with Garth Brooks on his Walkman, "I've Got Friends in Low Places." Movie Star says he's writing Amy to marry him as soon as he gets home.

We're laughing it up some now, coming back down now.

In my helmet I've got the picture of Lynn
by the toboggan.

I heat up MRE pork in barbecue sauce on
the grill at back of the tank.

Like last night was just some nightmare.

23

Bobby, I wrote him, *I'm surprised you even think about Lynn D., since . . .*

Bobby, I tried again, *the other night at the movies I saw your pen pal with some guy and . . .*

I was in Mr. Raleigh's class when I tried to write something to Bobby but couldn't.

Mr. Raleigh held a debate about whether or not Sinead O'Connor was right to skip the Grammy Awards in protest of the Gulf War. Does an entertainer have a right to bring politics into things? What about her statement that nothing can harm you when you speak the truth?

Ollie Burns said, "Yeah, but what *is* the truth? How the hell does a baldie rock star know what it is?"

"Do *we*?" Mr. Raleigh asked us. "Or is the information we're getting one-sided? We see videos of smart bombs hitting military targets, but none of stupid bombs hitting civilian buildings. Are we getting the truth from Baghdad?"

We booed him, except for Osborne de la Marin the Fourth, Kathy Wheat, and my date from the other night, Sloan Scott, who I found out was a liberal. She didn't believe in the death penalty, not even for sickos like Hannibal the Cannibal from *Silence of the Lambs*!

She let me kiss her good night at the door, but there was something strange going on, since she heaved this big sigh as though she'd thought she was kissing Christian Slater, then opened her eyes to see it was only Gary Peel.

I liked her looks and a certain sure way she had. I'd made up my mind, too, to get a life, so I asked her if she wanted to celebrate Dave's birthday Wednesday and she said she'd see.

When I got home from school, Mom was watching CNN, at the same time having a conversation with my father.

"You might as well hear this too, Gary," she said.

"Hear what?"

"Don't ask me how I know, but Lynn Dunlinger is in love with Bobby."

"How do you know?" my father said.

"Don't ask me that. I told you not to."

My dad said to Mom, "I *know* how you knew. You're up in Lingering Shadows working on those curtains and you've been snooping. I want to tell you something about what else *not* to do when you're up there."

"I don't snoop! I was looking for a scissors and I opened a drawer and there it was: this poem. I blushed reading it, I can tell you. It was all about waiting for the day they wouldn't have to be apart, and she could—I'm quoting now— she could be his loving lingering lover totally, or something to that effect. Her spelling's bad."

My father tried again. "I want to tell you something about what else not to do besides read her love poems when you're up there, Wanda . . . Mr. Dunlinger says you smoke up there."

"One. I smoked one cigarette."

"He says he was up there last night and he found a butt in a saucer of coffee."

"The rug men were up there, the uphol- sterer—it could have been anyone."

"It was a Camel. He knows it's your brand, Wanda."

118

"Other people smoke Camels. Jules Raleigh smokes them."

"Jules has no reason to be up there."

I stayed out of it.

"Just be warned," my father said.

"I think she wrote that for Valentine's Day, for Bobby," said my mother. "Did Mr. D. mention seeing *that*?"

"He only said to tell you he doesn't like smoking above the first floor in Linger."

"He obviously didn't see it then."

My father said, "She could have written that poem to anyone."

"Not *anyone* is away but Bobby. She never brings any boyfriends around, either, not anymore!"

"That's true," my father said.

Then he said, "Wouldn't that be something!"

"Our Bobby!"

"Well, don't write him any congratulations," I said.

"No, don't," said my father. "Let those two kids tell you in their own time."

"I wouldn't think of writing anything to him until he says something," said my mother.

I thought: Don't hold your breath.

My father said, "What's your long face about, Gary?"

"I know what it's about," said my mother.

"It's about having to go to work," I said.

"It's about your crush falling for your big brother," said my mother.

"Oh, sure, she's my crush."

"You always act shy around her, and you get a red face."

"Leave him alone," my father said. "He had a date the other night with Jack Scott's daughter, didn't he?"

"She's no Lynn Dunlinger, though," said my mother.

"Wanda, for Pete's sake, give the boy a break."

"You wonder why Bobby joined the army," I said.

"I like Sloan just the same," said my mother. "She's a very nice little girl."

My father said, "What the heck is Bobby going to do with Lynn Dunlinger? He didn't even finish high school."

"He doesn't need a diploma for what she has in mind," my mother said laughing.

I left my folks in fantasy land and headed up to Linger. In addition to busing weeknights, I was working two extra afternoons helping to set up, so I could afford to hear more of Sloan Scott's opinions on capital punishment and the Gulf War.

I didn't care that she was a liberal. Dating her made me realize I didn't have many strong feelings about anything. When she said, "What kind of a lawyer are you going to be—one of those corporate kinds who just go for the Wall Street money?" I said, "Well, I don't plan to fight for the rights of serial killers like Hannibal the Cannibal." But I couldn't give her a straight answer because I didn't know whose rights I'd fight for.

On the way home from that date, after we dropped the girls off, Dave Leonard said, "You want to make out? Say you're pro-choice, against all war, thinking of becoming a vegetarian, and very concerned about the environment."

"Some of it I am," I said.

"But all you talk about is Linger."

"Well, I work there."

"But it isn't the world, old buddy. This lady is the intellectual type. She reads and stuff."

"I read."

"She's the opposite of her old man, too. Sloan's into lefty politics, and she doesn't eat anything with a face. She's too deep. You want easy? Date Lolly Newman."

"I like Sloan all right."

"You're practicing safe sex in its purest form, Gary. No sex. I really don't think she'll come across at all, because she's got those principles. It's the reason *I* don't date her."

When I got up to Linger that afternoon, Mr. Dunlinger was setting up an end-of-the-war pool.

It cost five dollars to enter. You had to guess the day and the hour when the Gulf War would end.

He'd dragged out an old wishing well from the basement and draped an American flag over it. It was sitting in the front hall next to the packages for our servicepeople.

Jules was already at the piano in The Grill.

He was playing "Joan's Song," and the cat was sitting on the bar licking her paws, watching him. She and Lynn watched him the same way, practically drooling.

"Gary?" Mr. Dunlinger called out to me.

"Take a look here."

He was waiting for me, all smiles, under a hand-printed sign that said WISHING WILL MAKE IT SO!

Then I saw the reason, under the sign, in a frame on the well.

It was an old picture of Bobby, in his green and gold Linger waiter's uniform.

It said, *Linger proudly salutes its own alumnus Robert "Bobby" Peel, serving our country in Desert Storm.*

"I think we owe Bobby this," said Dunlinger. He was holding a Polaroid.

He said, "Get over here and let me take your picture next to it. You can send it to Bobby to show him we're behind him here at Linger."

I stood there while he pointed the camera at me, and Mr. Raleigh sang from the next room:

> *So linger awhile, let's see that smile,*
> *Secrets are mysteries still.*
> *You'll have your way, you will.*

24

"I saw your brother's picture in *The Berryville Record*," Sloan said. "By the wishing well at Linger?"

"Yeah." Mr. D. had never had to hire a public-relations man; he was better than any professional. "That's Bobby. . . . Didn't you ever see him before?"

"I think he waited on us a few times. My father loves going to Linger when he can afford to. It's a big deal to him, but not to me."

"Why don't you like it?"

"I don't eat that kind of food."

"That's right," I said.

Then I finally lunged at her.

We were in the back of Dave Leonard's Pontiac while Dave took a walk through the snow with Laura Greer. For his birthday she'd given him a bottle of Old Spice.

"Go easy," Sloan said.

There wasn't much leg room, so I was on my side, leaning into her, with my coat and gloves still on, even though Dave had left the motor running.

"Don't do that with your tongue," she said.

"Don't do what?"

"Don't flick your tongue like a snake at my lips."

"Forget it!" I said. I sat back and took off my gloves. I said, "Like a snake! Give me a break!"

"That's not the way to kiss," she said.

"You don't like someone to use his tongue?"

"I'm not talking about someone. I'm talking about you, Gary. You kissed me that way the last time, too!"

"Okay, okay, I won't use my tongue."

"You can use your tongue. Don't flick it."

"I didn't know I was flicking it."

"Let me show you something," she said. She leaned over and kissed me. She kissed me for a long time, long enough for me to imagine she was Lynn Dunlinger. I kept my eyes closed. I could hear Phil Collins singing "Another Day in Paradise." I thought, I'll say.

She finally said, "See?"

"Yes. I see," I said. I didn't even open my eyes. She was still right next to me. We kept kissing. I thought Ling was a good name. I wished I'd come up with that name for Lynn before he had.

Sloan finally sat back when we heard Dave and Laura coming toward the car.

She said, "What do you think about when you kiss me?"

"About you. What do you think about?"

"I won't tell you. I'd lie."

"Maybe I'm lying. Maybe I don't think about you."

"You shouldn't lie." She laughed.

I laughed too. There was some moonlight and she looked good. Her black hair fell to her coat collar, and she had on a white silk scarf and these gold loop earrings. Her eyes looked like she was enjoying being with me.

"You never said what you thought of the movie," she said.

We'd gone to see *Awakenings*, about some mental patients who were like zombies until they took a drug that brought them back to life for a while.

"I liked it," I said.

"That's the kind of man I'd like to marry," she said. "The doctor who did all that important research."

"I'd like to marry a woman like that," I said. I got that from Lynn, who was always saying women could do what men could, always making her father say chair*people* and service*people*.

"Wow, Gary! You're right!" Sloan said. "I should have said I'd like to *be* that kind of doctor, not that I'd like to marry that kind of doctor." She gave me this smile. "I didn't expect to hear that from you."

"I'm full of surprises," I said.

Dave opened the door and said, "You guys ready to go home? Laura has an eleven o'clock curfew." He stank of Old Spice.

Sloan said she had to be in by then, too. She'd taken off one of her gloves and put her hand in mine.

When I left her at the door, I said, "How about this Saturday? Do you want to see *The Grifters*?"

"Okay."

"Okay?" I laughed and we kissed, a quickie.

I went down her front walk feeling I'd left the

snake with the flicking tongue behind me.

Maybe I'd even left Lynn Dunlinger behind me.

Something had definitely happened to me that night.

"Like what?" Dave said when I told him something had.

"She didn't rattle me," I said.

I was laughing to myself: thinking rattlesnake.

"What's that grin for? Hey, Gary, did you make out?"

"I'm not going to tell you. I'd only lie."

Dave gave me a punch. "I thought you'd get a lecture on disarmament. I bet Laura, and she said no, it'd be on Planned Parenthood."

"What about you?" I said.

"She doesn't light my fire, Gary. I'm going for Lolly Newman this weekend."

"Easy does it," I said.

I was in a good mood when I got home.

I figured I'd get a Coke and go up and listen to some music in my room. I had the new Vanilla Ice album, *To the Extreme*. I might listen to Depeche Mode's *World in My Eyes*, too.

When I got inside the house, I could hear CNN blaring in the living room. It was all that was ever on anymore. What happened to Johnny Carson and Jay Leno?

I was going to sneak up to my room when Dad called out, "Come on in here, Gary. We're celebrating."

They had a bottle of Korbel champagne opened, and Mom raised her glass and grinned. "The war's over, Gary!"

25

About your pen pal, Lynn Dunlinger, I wrote
Bobby. *Today I saw her coming back from Lingering
Pines with this guy in the snow, and something about
the two of them was so different it's hard to describe,
but if I were you I wouldn't count on her, Bobby, if you
know what I mean.*

It was Friday afternoon around four, and the sun
was setting, so there was a sort of blue haze over
them. They were walking close together: Mr.
Raleigh going along in that awkward up-and-
down way he walked. She was looking up at him,
laughing, and just for a minute he stopped and
looked down at her, even though it was snowing
hard. Their coats were covered with it. He must
have said something, who knows what? But they
just stood there facing each other, and I think

anyone could tell what was with them.

Then he lurched back, picked up some snow in his gloves; and she saw he was making a snowball, so she did, too.

There wasn't any more to it than that: this big snowball fight began, and they were running toward Linger, laughing, she was chasing him, and it was hard for him in the snow, that was all.

But I never saw a moment frozen like that, one that said it all, except maybe in the movies, with violins swelling in the background, some kind of passionate symphony tipping off the stupid public that in case they didn't get it, this was something *hot* going on with these two.

I was watching out the kitchen window, my hands in soapy water, doing the pans because the cook wouldn't do cleanup and the guy that usually did was a no-show that day. He had a brother in Desert Storm and he'd been celebrating since the cease-fire.

Lynn had just gotten in from Faith Academy. I'd seen the taxi pull up some time ago. Her suitcase was still out in the hall near the wishing well.

The Dunlingers weren't there yet. They'd

gone to the Peace Celebration down at Holy Trinity.

What I didn't know, until dinner, was that my father had seen them too.

"Bobby's got some competition, is my bet," he said. "I saw Lynn Dunlinger frolicking in the snow with Jules Raleigh this afternoon, and they looked very much like a couple."

"A couple of what?" my mother asked.

"They looked like they were enjoying themselves," my father said, which was a lot like saying the Pope looked Catholic.

"Jules Raleigh may think they were enjoying themselves," my mother said, "but she's got only Bobby on her mind. You don't write a poem like that one day and the next day get interested in a clubfoot years older who plays piano in a bar."

My father winced. He said, "Wanda, Wanda."

"If Jules Raleigh'd had his way, Saddam Hussein would still be in Kuwait, and we wouldn't have anything to celebrate."

"That's right," I said. "A lot of people would still be alive, there wouldn't be oil spilling into the sea or oil-well fires mucking up the environment, and Bobby'd probably be down in Texas drinking beer with his buddies nights."

Walk with ducks and you start to waddle, I thought to myself. It wasn't Jules Raleigh at work on me, or Lynn either, because I'd been listening to them sound off through most of the war. It had to be a recent influence; the snake charmer herself, Sloan Scott.

"Tell that to Bobby when he comes home," my mother snapped. "Tell Bobby his little brother didn't appreciate what he did for his country."

Then my dad told us the head of Rotary, who'd won the end-of-the-war pool, was contributing his winnings to Linger for a party honoring all the servicepeople in the county.

He said, "Mr. D. said we'll wait for Bobby to come home to have it, though. Bobby's going to be the centerpiece!"

"That's wonderful!" my mother said. "I'm going to write Bobby tonight and tell him. It's going to make it a lot easier for Lynn and Bobby if Mr. D. approves."

My father said he didn't think Mr. D. knew anything about them.

"But don't tell me he'd object now," said my mother. "Bobby's coming home a hero!"

I'll never forget us sitting at that table, eating Mom's pot roast, having that discussion. Probably just as we'd sat down, the captain was picking up the phone and giving the overseas operator our number.

I remember when it rang I was going to answer, but my father got up because he didn't like my friends calling me during the meal. He'd tell them to call later.

I heard him say yes, he was Charles Peel, and then he gave this happy wave at us, pointing to the mouthpiece, expecting it to be Bobby.

Mom was on her feet when we heard him say, "Yes, Robert Peel is my son."

I felt for a minute the way I'd felt once when we were in Dave's car and we went into a skid, and the car began turning around, and we didn't know yet if we'd go over, hit a tree, hit another car; it was just very quiet and we were in this limbo for a few seconds, my heart caught in my throat.

"Then he's alive," my father said.

My mother was standing as close as she could get to the receiver, and my father put his arm around her.

"Thank God!" he said. "Thank you!" he said.

When he hung up, he said, "He's all right! He was wounded is all. He was wounded during a firefight with Iraqi tanks."

"Is he coming home?" My mother was crying.

26

We all thought the war was over, my brother said on the tape. *Some of the guys were sleeping in the back of the Bradley, since our day had begun at three A.M. I'd just finished an MRE and was writing in my notebook.*

Movie Star was up front driving. We had no idea we were heading into battle.

A guy beside Movie Star said, "Tracers." His voice was so calm. He was probably seeing a blaze of tracers in his thermal sights . . . and then he threw his radio headset down and shouted this time: "We're hit!"

We felt like we were being blown up and there was screaming and smoke, then red flames. The ammo aboard began exploding.

Movie Star was trapped in his seatbelt until the fire burned it away. Before he rolled out of there, he managed to unlock the ramp. That's how I got out.

He is burned badly. I am not that bad off, not like him, anyway.

Sugar took the force of the round and did not make it.

I will be in this hospital temporarily, then shipped out to one stateside. Mom and Dad, please don't plan to travel to where I am. I need time to recoup before we get together. I'll see you and Gary soon. Don't worry. Love you. 'Bye!

27

I am still trying to get in touch with Movie Star, my brother said on the tape. *Be sure and call me if any mail comes there for me. . . . The Army didn't tell you everything about that night, and that is okay too. There will be plenty of time to fill you in when I get home. I am doing fine although I have lost the hearing in my right ear, and my legs and back are healing slowly from the burns there. But I am improving fast, they tell me, so it won't be long now.*

"I wonder if he got my letter about Lynn Dunlinger yet," I said. "I wish I'd never mailed it."

I'd told Sloan everything. She was the only one I did tell. I'd gotten in the habit of going over to her house on Thursday nights to watch *Beverly Hills 90210.* Her mother would make strawberry Jell-O with bananas and miniature marshmallows on top. Between us we could eat five or six dishes of the stuff. Maybe we were trying to deaden our raging hormones.

Sloan said, "Do they forward mail from here to Saudi Arabia then back to Denver?"

Bobby was at Fitzsimmons Army Medical Center outside Denver, Colorado.

"Sure they do. But I don't know how long it'd take to catch up with him."

"What does he say to you on the phone?"

"We can't talk. Mom and Dad are there. He says to study, make good grades, stuff like that, stuff one of the cool, cool Peel brothers would never say."

"Can't you ask Lynn if she hears from him?"

"She hasn't. Not in a long time. She wrote him, though."

"Oh, she's all heart."

"It's not her fault. Ever since she heard he got wounded, she's felt rotten."

"She strung him along. She should."

"She didn't string him along. You don't understand."

From the living room we could hear Sloan's father laughing at something Rush Limbaugh had to say. It was his favorite radio program. Sloan's mother taped Rush every day so he could listen nights.

Sloan's father was a contractor whose business had slowed up because of the recession. He'd fought in Vietnam, and he said when he got back from "'Nam," he changed out of his uniform in the men's room at the San Diego airport so he wouldn't get dirty looks, that war was so unpopular.

When he wasn't talking about how thanks to Bush this country had finally learned how to kick ass, he was right there in the next room listening to Rush and keeping his eye on Sloan and me. We'd watch TV in the sun parlor. He was making sure nothing went on between us. He didn't know how much could go on when our eyes met, or our hands touched, or our bodies sat side by side. It wasn't sex and it was. By the time Saturday night rolled around, the backseat of Dave's Pontiac seemed as luxurious as a honeymoon suite with a round bed and a heart-shaped tub. We'd grab each other. It was sex and it wasn't.

Sloan said her father called feminists fema-Nazis. She was for nearly everything he was against. She said she was living proof conservative politics wasn't genetic.

Promptly at eleven P.M. Mr. Scott strolled in yawning, in case I didn't get the message that it was past everyone's bedtime.

He asked me, "When's the big blow-out for Bobby up at Linger?" He patronized Waffle Waffle more than he did Linger, but Linger was everyone's place for special occasions.

"Mr. Dunlinger says maybe he'll do it this summer. Whenever my brother gets home."

"Is your Mr. Raleigh going to play the piano?"

"Why is he Gary's Mr. Raleigh?" Sloan asked.

"He's your Mr. Raleigh too, isn't he? Isn't that where you pick up all your liberal ideas?"

"Gary's not a big liberal, Daddy."

I laughed. "I'm just a little liberal, I guess."

"When your big brother comes home, you ask him what *he* thinks of high school teachers who march in peace parades."

"I'll do that," I said. I had the idea he didn't like me, that the only points I got in his eyes were because Bobby'd been in Desert Storm.

"Ned Dunlinger ought to tell your Mr. Raleigh he doesn't belong in any victory celebration."

Mr. Scott was a big, beer-bellied roughneck who rode around in a Ford truck with his two black Labs barking in the back. Pete and Repeat, snoozing out in their doghouses that very moment.

When I left there nights, he had to stand on the porch and shout "Stay!" so they wouldn't eat through the back of my pants.

When Sloan was helping me into my coat, I told her to tell her mother thanks again for the Jell-O. When Mr. Scott was downstairs, Mrs. Scott was up, and vice versa. Before I knew that was always the way it was, I used to think they'd just had a fight.

Mrs. Scott seemed to claim the upstairs for her turf. Sloan said that was where her sewing room was, that because of the recession she was doing tailoring for the Berryville Dry Cleaners. Mr. Scott didn't want that broadcast, so I had to promise never to refer to it.

When she did appear, she was this thin little lady who seemed always to be running, the same way Edith Bunker did on the reruns of *All in the Family*. She'd ask if she'd made enough Jell-O, if we wanted some Mallomars, more Coke, anything so she could wait on us. She always thanked me for coming, when it should have been me thanking her for managing to raise a daughter as great as Sloan, with Bigfoot under the same roof.

I was falling hard for Sloan. I thought about that while I walked home that night. She had a theory that falling was the best part, and landing was the beginning of the end. She said her father had actually gotten down on one knee in the dining room of The Berryville Hotel, before it went to seed, and begged her mother to marry him. Look at them now, she said. They've landed.

Her idea was to avoid landing, which meant there was always that point when she'd stop us from going further.

"It's not safe, anyway," she said.

"We'll make it safe." For the first time in my life I was carrying a couple of Trojans in my wallet, just in case.

"I don't want it to happen when I'm so young. If it really bothers you, Gary, you'll have to date someone else."

There wasn't anyone else, anymore. I don't know how long it had been since I'd indulged in my favorite daydream of Lynn Dunlinger cornering me in some hallway up at Linger to tell me I'd been on her mind a lot. Then I'd say, What do you mean? and she'd say, You know what I mean, and the rest was X-rated.

I kept remembering her out in the snowstorm with Jules Raleigh, the way they looked at each other with the snow falling on them, and then that awkward up-and-down gait of his when he ran after her.

I wanted to write Bobby about Sloan, but I didn't think someone who'd come out of a war deaf and burned would be greatly thrilled by news that I'd lucked out while he was gone and finally found a life.

Even Mom and Dad weren't aware what was going on with me. I had the war to thank for that. I liked having my own private world. Bobby was the only one I'd talk to about Sloan, anyway, and I figured he'd come home and the cool, cool Peel brothers would get back their Sunday walks together, when we'd let Mom and Dad drive home from church. We'd pick up ice cream for Sunday dinner.

My letters to him were mostly about school and Linger. I told him how Mr. D. had made us replace all the old yellow ribbons with new ones, and there were huge American flags in every room, with a blowup of Bobby in his Linger uniform over the bar.

He'd started to count the days from the war's end to Bobby's return. It was up to Day 20, or something like that now. Mr. Yee changed the number every morning, and in the weekly ads for Linger, the number appeared with "Waiting for Sp.4 Robert Peel," after it (Bobby'd been promoted to Spec-Four). On one tape he said he was only a dozen more grades until brigadier. He'd also received a Bronze Star with a V for valor.

We worried some about what Bobby meant when he said that the Army hadn't told us everything. But we figured he was referring to all the details of the Battle of Norfolk, which was what they'd named this tank war in the desert.

Dad figured Bobby was sparing Mom the bloody details until he was healed and home, and Mom figured Bobby was sparing Dad.

Every time they hinted at how much they'd like to go out to Denver, just for a day even, just to see him, Bobby said he wanted to wait until he could come home.

When I got in that night, Mom and Dad were having a fight. I could hear them from downstairs. I could hear Dad shouting something that ended in "all your fault."

They didn't have bad fights very often, but sometimes Mom agreed with Bobby about Mr. Dunlinger's treatment of Dad. I remember Bobby used to say You work for a man for twenty-one years and you still call him Mister while he calls you Charlie!

I knew Dad had trouble standing up for himself, and I was embarrassed for him at times.

I made a lot of noise on the stairs going up to my room, so they'd know I was back in the house.

That worked.

They quieted down.

I heard some closet-door slamming and I heard a few muffled, angry words, but I put on C + C Music Factory's "Gonna Make You Sweat," and I danced around by myself, the only way I *could* dance, getting out of my clothes, getting with it. I was thinking how much easier dancing was when you had someone in mind you'd be moving toward, who'd be moving toward you, too.

It was my father's habit to take a cup of tea up to my mother first thing every morning, and he came down to do it the next day while I was pouring milk over my Froot Loops.

He said, "Do you know how much sugar's in there? Why don't you eat Special K instead? Or pay your own dentist bills!"

I chuckled. "Rough night, huh, Dad?"

"Jules Raleigh's in trouble, thanks to your mother."

"What'd she do to him?"

"Your mother was smoking again in Lingering Shadows and Mr. D. raised hell with her. So she got the bright idea to say she wasn't the only one who smokes Camels. She said someone else who's here all the time smokes two packs of Camels a day!"

"So what? Mr. Raleigh doesn't go up there. Dunlinger knows that."

"But it got him to go up there and look around good!"

My father slapped a bag of Celestial Seasonings Lemon Zinger on the counter.

"And?" I said.

"And he found a book Raleigh gave his daughter, with something written in it. I don't know what it was. But he came down the stairs with it in his hand and he watched Jules from a barstool. He just sat there watching him. Jules saw him watching him, so when he finished his set, he goes over and he says, 'What's up?' Mr. D. says, 'I know all about it. Lynn told me everything.'"

"What was that supposed to mean?" But I knew the trap had been set, and Mr. Raleigh probably walked right into it. That was his way: to take people at their word, to trust.

My father said, "Jules looked like the cat who'd swallowed the canary. He says to Mr. D., 'I'm relieved, Mr. D. I wanted to tell you myself.'"

I said, "Uh-oh."

"And Mr. D. punched him. Hard! Jules fell down on The Grill's floor. And Mr. D. said, 'Get out now! Don't come back here!' There were customers still there, Gary. I've *never* seen Mr. D. lose control like that." My father turned around and looked at me. "So we can thank your mother for opening up one whopper of a boil!"

"She didn't know it, Dad."

"But if she just hadn't made that insinuation! . . . See, I must have been right, son. Remember when I said I saw them that afternoon, and they looked like a couple?"

28

Bobby
c/o Linger
Berryville, Pennsylvania

Dear Bobby,

I do not know your last name, nor even if you will
ever receive this. Your first name and the name of the
restaurant came to me in letters from my son, Donald
Sweet, who served with you in the Gulf War.

Since his mother died when he was very young, my
boy and I grew closer than most fathers and sons. I
took him with me everywhere until this war sepa-
rated us.

I am anxious to know anything you can tell
me about his last days and his death. I am taking
the chance that you are alive, and that this will be

received by you, if it is, with a compassionate spirit, since Donny was my only boy, and I wish to find out anything I can about the end of his life.

I will be grateful to you for any information.

Sincerely,

Spencer Sweet

29

Friday night I waited tables at Linger because a regular weekend waiter came down with flu.

That weekend was the first one since Christmas that Lynn hadn't come home from boarding school.

Neither was Jules Raleigh behind the piano at Linger, though he'd been at school that morning with a black eye. Word was out that he'd had a fight up at Linger, but no one knew any details.

Sloan was the only one I'd told the truth.

The kids thought he'd crack a joke about his shiner, but he didn't. He was in a foul mood. It didn't help that he was having more trouble than usual walking.

For homework he told us to write an essay about how the war had changed things. "Or how it *hasn't* changed things," he said. "Did it change anything in *your* life? Was it over before it could?

Whose lives do you think it changed? And what will happen now? Will everything just go back the way it was? What about Iraq? Do you have any idea what life is like there? Or doesn't that concern you? Should it? Let's hear your thoughts!"

Mr. Dunlinger had managed to find a middle-aged, crew-cut piano player who seemed to know only songs from the sixties, so we heard Beatles songs and things like "Lay Lady Lay," "Mellow Yellow," "Stop in the Name of Love," and "Surfer Girl."

Mrs. Dunlinger got up and sang "Yester-me, yester-you, yesterday."

When Mr. D. asked the piano player if he knew anything "patriotic," all the fellow could come up with was "Soldier Boy" and "Give Peace a Chance."

"Not 'Give Peace a Chance!'" Mr. D. barked at him. "Never play that hippies' song here!"

The Regency Room didn't have the same feeling without the violin playing, and everyone was asking for Jules.

"I don't know where he is." Mr. Dunlinger shrugged.

My father looked grim and uncomfortable

and went home as soon as the dinner crowd left.

I had the same ominous feeling Mr. Yee seemed to have when he told me, "We've seen the last of Jules around here."

"Is that what Mr. D. said?"

"No, he said nothing. I just know it."

Even Joan felt the change, I think, and she hightailed it out the door, down to the highway. Someone stopped his car and found the Linger collar around her neck, and brought her up wrapped in a newspaper.

Mrs. D. said when the ground thawed they would bury her out in her hunting ground in Lingering Pines.

I got home late, and Mom was watching a movie she'd rented with Goldie Hawn in it called *Swing Shift*.

She said, "Exactly what Lynn did to Bobby with Jules Raleigh, Goldie did to Ed Harris with Kurt Russell! Exactly! Only in this film poor Ed came home on leave and found out for himself. . . . I don't know how Bobby's going to handle it, but we're not going to tell him now."

I didn't care to point out everything all over

again: that the poem she'd seen in Lynn's bureau drawer was obviously meant for Mr. Raleigh, not Bobby, that Mom had manufactured the whole thing out of that, that and wishful thinking.

I told her about Joan, and she got teary-eyed and said that cat had been there sixteen years and now an era had ended.

"No more mouse corpses in The Regency Room," I said.

She shouted the news down to my father. He was tinkering with something in his workshop, a part of the basement Bobby used to call "The Land of Buried Dreams." Bobby said whenever Dad wanted to put something behind him, he went down there and nailed an old chair together, or glued a handle back on an old teapot—anything to deny something in his own life had come apart. I never knew before how much he'd liked Jules Raleigh. He hated it that Mom got him sacked.

The next day Mom and I called Bobby and told him about Mr. Sweet's letter, and he asked us to read it to him.

When Mom was finished doing it, she went outside where Dad was shoveling snow, to tell him we had Bobby on the phone.

It was the first time I had any privacy to talk to him.

He said, "Is anyone else listening?"

"No."

"Do you remember me writing about Sugar?"

"Sure!"

"When we got him out of the Bradley and laid him down on the ground, he was screaming. His feet were gone, Gary, and his left arm. I could see white bones and shoulder ligament where it had been. He got the worst of one of the tank rounds."

I mumbled something, I don't remember what.

Mom was back, calling out "Tell Bobby about Joan, honey!"

"Is that what the Army didn't tell us?" I asked him.

"Later, on the floor of the tank? We found his feet still inside his combat boots, sliced from his shins."

Mom took the receiver from me and said, "Joan got hit by a car, Bobby. She was sixteen years old! The place just won't be the same without that darn cat!"

30

Monday morning there was a sub for Mr. Raleigh.

She wrote her name on the chalkboard: Mrs. Burke. She said she was from Torrington, which was a town seven miles away. She had on a blue blazer with a shorter skirt than most of our teachers wore, and you could tell she wasn't used to teaching because her heels were really high. She had to either sit down all day or spend the night soaking her feet.

When someone asked her where Mr. Raleigh was, she said she didn't know, she didn't know him, but she would very much like someone to volunteer to read his homework assignment.

Osborne de la Marin's hand shot up instantly. He said, "I wrote mine in verse."

"Very original." She smiled.

So Osborne got up and stood there with his

long black braid down the back of his red
Tommy Hilfiger shirt, and he read his poem.

> *How DARE Mr. Saddam march into Kuwait,*
> *Driving up oil prices, something we hate!*
> *Incubator babies thrown to the floor?*
> *Reason enough to march off to war!*
>
> *Smart bombs sail over dark sands at night,*
> *CNN reports are filled with delight!*
> *Dumb bombs behind them in Bagdad explode.*
> *Civilians are slaughtered, but we are not told.*
>
> *Anyway, we're killing silly old Iraqis,*
> *Dish towels on their heads, tackiest of tackies.*
> *Vietnam is over, we're back in the clover!*
> *Out of our war cammies, into our pajammies.*
>
> *If Saddam is still there,*
> *Why on earth should we care?*
> *We have met our fate*
> *And oil's well in Kuwait.*

There was some scattered applause, one
whispered shout of "Faggot!" and more groans
of disgust and disapproval.

Mrs. Burke simply said, "Next?"

31

On Good Friday, just before we got the afternoon off, it was announced on the intercom that Mr. Raleigh had resigned, "effective immediately."

No reason was given. Everyone I knew thought it was because the school board felt he was brainwashing us.

There were petitioners waiting outside, kids singing "All we are say-ing is give Jules a chance!" and even a few faculty members carrying signs that said things like "Heil B.H.S.!" and "Free Speech?"

It was sleeting and blowing out. Sloan and I got under her battered old umbrella with SUCK MY KISS written across it and started down the front walk, coat collars up, gloves on, eyes pelleted by the frozen rain.

That's why we didn't see the long black Lincoln Town Car, lined up with the others that were always there at the end of a school day. The gold Linger logo was on the side door.

We finally heard its horn. Then I saw Lynn inside.

Sloan said, "She's been waiting for you, Gary. Go with her. I don't care."

"No, stay here a sec."

I ran around to the driver's side trying to duck the wet needles on my neck.

Lynn had on a black-leather bomber jacket and a black baseball cap with DKNY in white letters. Her long hair was tucked under the cap. There was a white silk scarf around her neck, and she smelled of that perfume she always wore.

She had on shades, too. I'd never known her to wear them. I didn't know anyone who'd wear them in that weather.

"Would you come with me to Flynn's, Gary?"

"Can I bring Sloan? You know Sloan Scott, don't you?"

"No, I don't, but I don't care. Bring her."

Back on the sidewalk Sloan said, "I'm not even dressed, Gary."

"You're not even *dressed*?"

"I look awful today, and look at her."

"She's got a baseball hat on, for God's sake, Sloan. I think she's been crying, too."

We squeezed into the front and Lynn started in as soon as we got through the introductions.

She said her father'd forced Mr. Raleigh to resign, and it was all done behind her back, starting with Mr. Raleigh calling her to say he wouldn't be there last weekend and not to come home. He was packing his things up, at Flynn's.

"Daddy sat on him, Gary, until he said 'uncle.' He told Jules that everyone on the school board was in Rotary with him, that I was underage, and that he'd see to it Jules never taught again—*anywhere*—if he didn't turn in his resignation."

"What proof did your father have of anything?" I asked her.

"Daddy makes his own proof . . . and he has the book. It's my fault for forgetting to take the book back to school with me. As it is, I hid it under my sweaters, but old eagle eye found it."

"What was the book?" Sloan said.

"It was just poetry. e.e. cummings. But Jules circled something that sounds like we were lovers, *that way*, and we never were. Then he wrote the page number in the front, and he wrote, 'For my

Lingerling with love from J-Bird.' I mean, my Gawd, that's embarrassing, incriminating, corny . . . and all Daddy needed!"

"How did you find out your father threatened Jules that way?"

"I found out because Daddy told me. He loves to gloat, loves to say things like Well, your Mr. Right was wrong about a lot more than the war, wasn't he? He didn't waste any time clearing out, did he? He knows better than to get into a contest with *me*. . . . I'll have him up on morals charges if he shows his face around here again— you're a minor!"

She shoved a tape in.

It was Whitney Houston's "All the Man That I Need."

We were doing sixty-five in a thirty-mile-an-hour zone.

"I love this song," Sloan said.

"I don't love going this fast," I said. "And you better take it easy, Lynn. We're down near Railroad Avenue, and the homeless are around there. All you need is to run over someone!"

"They're not sleeping in the streets yet!"

I'd never seen her so hyper. She was actually stepping on the gas.

She said, "Where did he ever get the idea to search my room?"

Sloan poked my appendix with her elbow as if to say Don't tell her about your mother; now is not the time.

I was thinking I'll tell Lynn about my mother the day Dunlinger invites Nine Inch Nails to play in The Regency Room. There was no way Lynn was going to believe anything I told her, once she found out it was my mother who'd tipped Mr. Raleigh, never mind how accidentally.

She'd never believe I wasn't to blame.

I decided to change the subject, fast. "What are you going to do at Flynn's?"

"That's where you two come in. You tell Mrs. Flynn you're his students, and you want to write him. I know she'll have a forwarding address."

"You don't know where he is?"

"Gary," she said, pushing the car up to seventy, "I didn't take Daddy's car without his knowing it and drive down to your school and wait a half hour out front, and now find myself heading down to Allen Avenue in the freezing damn wind and sleet, because I know where he is. If I knew where he was, I'd probably be with him, wouldn't you say?"

"Yes, I'd say," Sloan said.

"I'd say so too," I said. "I just hope we get there in one piece."

Sloan was nudging me, and I was rubbing my knee against hers, but this was not hormones driving us, it was adrenaline; it was a cry to survive from our pores in the form of sweat, the word we never say in the Peel house.

"Don't you think you'd better park down the street so Mrs. Flynn doesn't see the Linger car?" I said.

"I thought of that. Daddy's probably promised her a year of free dinners if she keeps her mouth shut. I'm not going in. I'll park a few doors away."

She went around a corner with the wheels squealing, the sleet whooshing against the windshield, and Whitney Houston hitting a long, sweet, high note I figured might be our swan song.

"I wish I had a piece of paper," I said to Sloan.

"Why?"

"I'd write down my last wishes. I'd say If I die in a car wreck, don't have a celebration of my life instead of a funeral. You know how they have nothing but celebrations these days?"

"Yes?"

"I don't think it's anything to celebrate, death in a car crash at sixteen."

"You *liar*," Lynn said. "You told me you were two years younger than Bobby, not three."

"That was way back when you obsessed me," I said. "Back before I knew how you drive."

Sloan was laughing into her hands.

I was thinking how I'd always liked the way the Lincoln smelled, that great new expensive-car smell of good leather. Even the chrome smelled.

But did I want it for my casket?

Finally, Lynn slowed up.

She said, "We're almost here, I think. There's Waffle Waffle down the street."

"You better park here," I said.

"It kills me!" Lynn said. "e.e. cummings! I don't even like him, the way he printed his name in lower case, all that 'your hands are like the rain' crap! It was so phony! I couldn't tell Jules I'd rather read Leonard Cohen!"

"Park," I said. "Slow up so you can park, Lynn."

"To have e.e. cummings do me in!" she said.

"The irony of it!"

"'Lingerling' and 'J-Bird' did you in," I said. "Those are lovers' names for each other."

Lynn said, "Ned Dunlinger did us in," and she said it between her teeth, suddenly braking, teaching us as we lurched treacherously toward the windshield the value of the seat belts we didn't have fastened.

32

Dear Roberto,

My name is Gina Sanchez, and I am Augustin's sister.

I feel like I know you because of what he has written home about you. Then you and Sugar signed the card Augustin sent me for my quinceanera. Do you remember that?

I am sorry to hear that Sugar died. Our whole family feels terrible over that news.

We also hope you are having a good recovery.

Now I must tell you about Augustin, Roberto (does it bother you to call you that? Do you like Robert better?). You see, he had some very, very bad things happen. I will just have to tell you straight out. Some of it you may know.

What has happened is that Augustin has been so badly burned, he does not look the same. One eye, his nose and lips and ears have all been burned away. Six

166

*fingers are gone, his thumbs, and the skin on his legs
and one arm.*

*He is now undergoing plastic surgery and skin
grafts.*

*Roberto, we know you have been burned, too, but
not so bad, you say, and so I think you did not realize
all that was burned on Augustin.*

*I am asking you now not to call him by the nick-
name you fellows called him by over there. He does not
look a lot like a movie star now.*

*Some of his friends from high school called him
Gus.*

*The family has always called him Augustin or
Gustin.*

*He has asked me to write you and give you his ad-
dress, and fill you in on his damage.*

*Right now we do not know when he will be up and
about, but a nurse or one of us writes letters for him.
He has received all yours, and I know he will like to
see more.*

*I hope someday we meet you. We have heard about
your Linger and it sounds good.*

Yours truly,
Gina Sanchez

33

"My mother's down at Waffle Waffle," the kid said. "She eats early, then goes to Caldor's to work until nine."

"We just want to ask you about Mr. Raleigh," I said.

The kid invited us in and said his name was Marty Flynn.

He was wearing a baseball cap backward, and a T-shirt that featured Mr. Happy Face with a bullet hole through his forehead, blood trickling over the smile.

He said to Sloan, "I like your umbrella. I like The Red Hot Chili Peppers."

"I'm not into them—someone gave it to me," said Sloan.

"'Suck My Kiss' is a big mosh tune," he said. "I'm into mosh." He was about fourteen.

I said, "We're students of Mr. Raleigh's."

"You mean you *were*."

"Yeah, we were. He left so fast, we didn't get a chance to return a book we have of his."

Sloan said, "Plus we'd like to say good-bye to him."

"We don't have any address for him, so I'm sorry."

"Your mother doesn't?"

"I said *we*. We're the only two here. He made three."

"What if someone wants to reach him?"

The kid shrugged and shifted his weight from one Doc Martens to the other.

He said, "He paid up through June, so *we* don't have to reach him."

"What about other people?" Sloan asked him.

"What about them?"

"Where does he live?" Sloan asked him.

"He did live here. He didn't have two places."

"Do you know where his son is?"

"He's in some school in Vermont."

"That's right. Vermont," I said. "I remember he went there one weekend."

"All we know is he said he resigned and he wouldn't be back."

"Okay." I zipped my jacket back up.

He said, "We heard he got kicked out for opposing the war."

"Something like that," I said.

We were opening the door on our way out.

"My mom was for the war, and I was against it. But she says there was no reason to can him."

"I was against it too," Sloan said.

We walked down the street in the rain. "What's mush?" I asked her.

"Mosh. M-O-S-H. It's sort of like slam dancing."

"What's slam dancing?"

"I knew you were going to say that."

"I don't dance. Bobby doesn't either. We Peel men don't dance."

"That's got to change. I love to."

"Maybe you should date Marty Flynn. Did you see that T-shirt?"

"Yeah, but deep down he's a peacenik," she said.

Lynn was playing Janet Jackson's "Love Will Never Do."

She said to get in back since we were wet. I told her we didn't have any luck.

I said, "But at least we found out his son's school is in Vermont."

"You think I don't know that?"

"I guess you do," I said. "Come to think of it."

"Come to think of it, I've been there!" Lynn said.

"I didn't know you were there."

"The Willow School in Montpelier. We went there. Then we went tobogganing."

I remembered the weekend he went tobogganing.

"You saw his son?" Sloan said.

"I saw him. What there is to see. He doesn't recognize anybody, can't speak, can't do anything for himself. He's five going on three months."

"I feel so sorry for Mr. Raleigh," said Sloan.

Lynn had started up again. We were up to forty in a twenty-mile zone, heading around a corner past a STOP.

The first time I realized Lynn was crying was when Sloan passed her a Kleenex.

"Thanks," Lynn said. "I guess I've got to try and get his address through Willow."

"Sure," I said.

"That's not going to be easy. They know I'm

not related. They're very strict about who gets what information up there. I've already made one try."

"We're way past the speed limit," I said.

She reached beside her and tossed back a manila envelope. "I've been meaning to give this to you, Gary."

"What is it?"

"Maybe someday anything to do with the Gulf War will be historic. And probably Bobby would like those."

I opened it and peeked inside. "You don't want them?" I said.

"What are they?" Sloan asked me.

"They're all of Bobby's letters," Lynn said. "Someday he might appreciate having them."

"Someday," I said.

"I didn't give them to your mother because I figured she'd think I was this heartless bitch, giving back the letters her soldier son wrote me."

"You figured right. I wouldn't say anything to her, either, if I were you."

"They're not like love letters or anything."

"Well, he hardly knew you."

"It's funny, isn't it? All the times I saw him

172

around Linger, I can't remember having one conversation with him. I thought he thought I was spoiled."

"You?" I said.

"Spoiled?" I said.

34

April 10, 1991

Dear Mr. Sweet,

   Your letter was forwarded to me. I'm Robert Peel, and as you know your son and I were buddies in Bravo Company, in Operation Desert Storm.

   I am recovering now, and on my way home soon. Yours is the first letter I am writing myself since the war, for I have had to ask the nurses or volunteers to help me write or tape.

   We called your son Sugar. We is me and Augustin Sanchez, who is also on the mend in a hospital in New Jersey. We called him Movie Star.

   You would maybe like to know Sugar didn't die without getting a few of them personally. We all got a lot of them firing at them or running over them, but on the first night in the Iraqi desert, after a breach and attack with eighty Iraqis and their commander surrendering to us, we were resting up when we saw these dismounts come into our thermal sights.

A bad sandstorm had started up. We could see only 200 or 300 meters ahead with the naked eye, but we could see 900 meters ahead with the thermal sights. And there were these dismounts. Those are dismounted infantry men, maybe spies, or maybe armed with rocket-propelled grenades: tiny targets that show up in a visual, Nintendo-like TV image, and these three would move, stay still, move, stay still in this little dance on the black-and-green screen we watched.

Sugar didn't want to kill them. He had blown up tanks and run over those in trenches, but not loners like this. He asks the Lt. Col. could he fire ten meters to the left? And he does and they're coming. You never know if they're out to surrender, because most of them up close are. So he hits near the right now.

Then we see them headed toward a Bradley, and Sugar says he's going to blast their asses.

The thermal sights pick up heat, and when these guys got it, we watched the bodies go from green to black, meaning they were cold/dead.

He was a good friend, always making us laugh, singing us songs he made up, reciting poems, telling us about Kuwait and his life before the Army.

When he got it, Sugar bore the brunt of a Silver Bullet, a Sabot that only one of our Abrams fires.

Officially, so far, the Army says he died in a fire-fight with Iraqi tanks, but it was "friendly fire," a not-uncommon occurrence in this or any other war.

I am sure the Army will make a correction ultimately.

He deserved his Purple Heart, and I will never forget him. Please accept my deepest sympathy.

Sincerely,
Robert Peel

35

I came in from a cold April rain, dripping on the floor of Linger's lobby, Mr. Yee yelling at me, "Hey, you go around to the back. We just did these floors!"

"I have to give this to Mrs. D."

It was the new Kitty Kelly biography of Nancy Reagan. I'd picked it up from The Berryville Library for her.

"I'll give it to her."

"Let me."

She was always good for five dollars when you went out of your way to do her a favor.

"You're money mad," Mr. Yee said.

Then I noticed he had Bobby's picture under his arm.

"Where are you going with my brother?"

"I'm putting him back here in the lobby."

"How come?"

"Mr. Dunlinger says it's not right in the bar."

Above Bobby's head the sign said Day 46.

Mr. Yee said, "Mr. Dunlinger thinks it's depressing. The war is over now, officially. Your brother could be another two, three months."

"Why isn't it depressing in the hall then?"

"People don't drink in the hall. We had fights starting about the war. We had the ones who said we should have gone in and got Saddam Hussein, and the ones who said not another one of our boys' lives was worth that. . . . Then there were some fights starting about Jules, why he isn't here anymore."

"Does anyone know the real reason?"

Mr. Yee looked at me. "The real reason?"

"What the fight with Mr. D. was about?"

"It was about Mr. D. not being able to take his talk about the war. About what we did to Iraq."

Mr. Yee looked right into my eyes. He'd been there the night Dunlinger fought with Jules. He *knew*, but he wasn't letting on that he did.

He said, "We're going to put the picture in here. Maybe it'll stop arguments."

He hung Bobby's picture near the wall thermostat.

I waited on the doormat until I wasn't dripping wet, and then I went down the hall and knocked on Mrs. D.'s door.

She was drinking a cup of tea. She'd moved her white wicker chaise down from Lingering Shadows. Her face brightened when I put the book down on her desk.

"Did you hear Nancy Reagan consulted astrologers and then told President Reagan what he should do?"

"I heard something like that."

"I liked Ronnie, though. He always made me feel good when I'd see him getting out of the helicopter on the White House lawn. He always touched her, always."

She was going into her purse, getting out her wallet.

Sloan and I had finally worked out a deal about dating. We went Dutch, but we could also treat each other to something special.

She was teaching me to dance, *with* someone instead of up in my room by myself, and she'd gotten me the new Enigma album that included "Sadeness Part I."

So I got her Mariah Carey's, with "Someday" on it.

Mrs. Dunlinger passed a five across to me and said, "And thank you for not spreading the gossip, Gary. Lynn tells me you know about everything."

"Yes, Ma'am."

"I will never forgive Jules."

I didn't say anything.

"I'm sorry if Bobby got the wrong impression, too. That's also unforgivable."

"Lynn didn't do anything, really."

"Lynn never *does* anything, but things seem to happen because of her." She shoved a large sheet of paper across her desk and said, "What do you think of this?"

It was an ad layout.

NO, WE DON'T HAVE DOGGIE BAGS AT LINGER!

"Since when?" I said.

"Read on," she said. "This is my husband's newest idea, and I think it's his best."

No, we don't, and we're sorry.

We have Take Homes, instead, for we believe there shouldn't be any waste at a time when we have our homeless right down on Railroad Avenue . . . at a time when even those of us with homes are saving up to put our kids through college or take that well-deserved vacation down South (see America first!).

We encourage you to take everything home (except the silver, please). Maybe you'll drop off one of our T.H.'s to someone without a roof over his head, on your way home, or maybe late at night you'll have a family picnic in the kitchen. (Fido might even get a bite, after all.)

So ask for a Take Home. We'll add an extra roll, an extra cookie—something to surprise you, and make you glad you came to LINGER.

I looked up at her and she smiled. "Like it, Gary?"

"Yes, Ma'am."

"My husband thinks it's time people felt good about themselves again. Winning the war was the start of something. Now we'll feed our own people and we'll get back to old family values."

Then she said, "Wait until you see what we've planned for Bobby for his Fourth of July party!"

"If he's home by then."

She dug into her purse again.

"Look," she said.

She handed me a postcard from Denver.

Dear Mr. and Mrs. D.,
*   Can't wait to see those fireworks!*
*   Sincerely,*
*   Bobby*

36

Dear Roberto,

How about this beautiful, new handwriting of mine, hmmmm?

All your letters are greatly appreciated.

When I get out of here, I will be actually writing you with a few of my toes, this is for real! They are sewing them on my hands.

Maybe they should sew my foot in my mouth—since I told my father how we got hit, I think he is ready to bomb Bush or something like that.

Hey, guess who is my secretary? Someone who wants to meet you after all she's heard of you. That's right, my Amy.

She has not missed a day here, and even her old man has come to see me, too. She says Hey, don't call him an old man. Someday he's going to be our kids' grandfather, and then you can call him that.

I would like to see you, yes. We can do that when I

get all this surgery completed. Maybe I'll even get time off in between. I would like to meet Lynn, too, and have us all together.

But you never say how you are. How are you, Roberto?

Do you want to learn to dance yet?

Your good pal,
Gus Sanchez

37

It was a Monday afternoon in early June, and Bobby was expected home that evening.

Mom and Dad had gone into Philadelphia to get him. I worked at Linger after school, nervous and excited at the thought of seeing him.

I filled up a T.H. bag with leftover pasta from the kitchen, dropped in some Caesar salad, rolls, and a few Tollhouse cookies, and went over to Sloan's.

Her father was down at the American Legion, watching the ticker-tape parade in New York City for General Schwarzkopf and the troops.

"This is a little dessert in the spirit of celebration," said Mrs. Scott. She was carrying in Jell-O, red raspberry, with the little white marshmallows on top of some blueberries.

She said she had to let out some pants for the Berryville High Marching Band, who were playing at Linger after the Fourth of July Victory Parade downtown.

Bobby was being featured in the parade. Then Linger was having the big party in his honor.

"I hope he likes me," said Sloan. "What if he doesn't?"

I said not to worry, he'd like her. She was beside me on the rug in the sunroom. She had on some new stuff: white cotton jeans with a gold chain belt, a gingham blouse and pink leather cowboy boots. She'd started wearing perfume ever since I'd talked about Lynn's. She wore something called Patchouli.

We were watching MTV and doing homework. Axl Rose was prancing around the stage barechested with his tattoos up and down his arms, in red-white-and-blue stars-and-stripes tight shorts. Slash was dancing around him with his hair in his eyes, working his guitar.

I was trying to cram for my final French exam, and Sloan was doing an essay called "Could Economic Sanctions Have Worked in Ousting Iraq from Kuwait?"

It was guaranteed not to be read aloud by Mrs. Burke, who had Mr. Raleigh's job permanently now and steered far away from any political discussions.

We'd work, watch, break for a hot clinch; work, watch, break. When we heard the Labs barking, we ran to the door, afraid someone passing would be bitten.

Sloan was saying, "I thought Daddy took them with him."

We stood in the open doorway as Pete and Repeat leaned their paws against the Linger Lincoln, parked at the curb.

Lynn didn't want to come in; she wanted to drive around. And Sloan wanted to finish her paper.

I said I'd take a ride with her if she'd drop me off. I expected the family back with Bobby around eleven.

"I found him," she said. "He was in Vermont, after all. I went up there last weekend. Daddy thought I was in Boston with my roommate."

She had on that same DKNY baseball cap pulled down on her forehead, a short black-leather skirt, and a white T-shirt.

I said, "Well? What happened?"

"He's got this tacky room on the first floor of

this place, and he came to the door when I rang his bell, and he just looked at me. I said can I come in, and guess what he said? He said 'I suppose so.' Do you believe that?"

"I believe anything."

"'I *suppose* so,' Gary."

She wasn't in a mood to drive fast, and I was glad of that.

I liked the smell of the car, and the beginning-of-summer aromas: the lawns coming in, the trees blossoming. It was finally dark, but there was a moon.

I said I was sorry. What else could I say?

"He said he realized it was all a mistake, and he said he was totally to blame. I said I want some of that blame, if the big sin was we fell in love." She shook her head. "Then he just about killed me. He said he was just lonely. He said it wasn't even close to love. He said I was infatuated like a schoolgirl, and he was bored and lonely."

"Maybe he was making that all up."

"His eyes were ice cold."

"Yeah."

"It was hideous, too, because he didn't have on his built-up shoe. He had to hobble around.

He was embarrassed, I think. He looked so . . . crippled."

"He is."

"He never seemed that way. . . . You're the only one I can talk to. I could have talked in front of Sloan, too, but I'm glad you came out with me."

"I have to be home in time for Bobby's arrival."

"I heard he was coming tonight. All of Linger's excited."

"So am I. I haven't seen him in ten months."

"Isn't it funny, Gary? Jules and I lasted about as long as that war did."

"Yeah."

"It was like we had our own Desert Storm."

We didn't say anything for a while.

We drove around.

There was a line of kids at McDonald's. They were interviewing for the summer night shift.

School would be out in a few weeks.

Lynn said, "I don't believe him when he says he was just bored! How could he say that?"

"Maybe he's afraid your father will bring him up on charges, Lynn."

"My father *would*, too, but we were *alone*, Gary. He could have said I love you but we can't be together."

"Would you have accepted that?"

"No."

Then she went over it all again, how she'd rung the bell, how he'd said he supposed she could come in, the cold blue of his eyes, how he'd said he'd been bored, the bare foot, how shriveled and white it was. She'd never seen the bad foot.

Then she was quiet, and then she went over it all again.

I wondered if any girl would ever feel that way about me, because I doubted Sloan ever would, even if I turned around, went back to her house, and told her it was finished, I needed sex, good-bye.

I think she'd have said you suck, anyway, Gary . . . or something close to that.

I wondered if I'd ever get into anything deeper someday, and I remembered when I'd stand up in Lingering Shadows and spray Red around and wish for a dark, lethal love.

Lynn thanked me for putting up with her, and

she said she was going to be a counselor that summer at that camp where they spoke only French. She was going to leave for there in a few days.

We pulled in front of my house, and I got out, wished her luck, and started up the walk.

My eye caught something to my left, coming down the street, limping along, and I thought, My God, it's him: Jules Raleigh.

But he was on a cane, and as he got closer, under the streetlight, I could see the wire of the hearing aid going down his shirt, and I could see the side of his neck that was bright red and swollen, with a scar that spread to his ear, pulling it closed.

He said my name, and he said something about his plane landing early, and he said he'd gone out for some ice cream.

"What flavor?" I said.

Because we were the cool, cool Peel brothers, the ones who didn't dance, or blubber the way I was doing when I grabbed him.

38

On my birthday, July 2, I got my driver's permit. On the Fourth, Dad let me take his Dodge Dart to drive Bobby up to Linger after the parade.

The day began with the church bells pealing, and then the First Presbyterian carillon played songs like "Faith of Our Fathers" and "The Battle Hymn of the Republic."

Before the parade everyone was invited to a thanksgiving service at Temple Emmanuel.

The mayor had asked citizens to hold off on fireworks until that evening, but we could hear firecrackers popping in the distance as we came out of the temple.

Bobby refused to ride around on a float, and they put him up front in a Chevrolet convertible the town supervisor was driving.

The school bands followed it, and clubs like Rotary, Elks, Lions, American Legion, and Veterans of Foreign Wars marched next, with their banners and floats.

Sloan's father was marching in his old Army greens with some other Vietnam vets, shouting as a cadence:

> *We're standing tall,*
> *We're looking good,*
> *We ought to be in Hollywood.*
> *One—two—three—four.*

The "Hollywood" made me think of Bobby's pal Movie Star, the only missing piece in a perfect celebration. Bobby said we couldn't expect someone in his shape to make the trip on a crowded weekend.

He said he'd see Sanchez on his way back through New York. Bobby had one more stint in a rehab hospital to endure before he got his discharge.

My brother was even getting along with Mr. Dunlinger. He said one thing the war had taught him was to let go of excess baggage. If you don't need it, don't carry it around.

After the parade, Mom and Dad joined the throng walking from center town up to Linger.

Bobby and I were in one of the few cars heading up Highland Hill. People seemed to want to soak up the sun and exercise en masse. Berryville looked like a town invaded by a marathon, only everyone was walking instead of running.

In the distance Linger was shining like some great castle festooned with flags. The Berryville High Marching Band was assembled on the porch, piping everyone into the buffet in Bobby's honor.

Bobby was in one of his good moods that day. Sometimes he was angry and depressed, but not that day. He even wore his uniform, when he'd said he wouldn't, originally. I think he did it for Mom and Dad, and for Linger, too. Everyone wanted to get in the spirit of things: welcoming home the war hero and all. How could they do it if the hero was in civvies?

Dunlinger had a special table for the press. They'd come from all over Philadelphia. Some with TV cameras, some ready for live remotes. There was a representative from *People* magazine there, too, plus an ABC unit from New York and a representative from *The Phil Donahue Show* looking things over.

Berryville had never seen anything like it.

In the car my brother said, "I hope I didn't keep Lynn from enjoying this. I hope she didn't make an early departure because of me."

"She's at camp."

"She's still going to camp?"

"She's a counselor now."

We hadn't talked about her at all. The first night he was home, he told all of us he didn't want to.

Now he said, "She was a great fantasy. When I was a kid I couldn't even look closely at her. I never knew what she had on. I couldn't face her, I thought she was so fantastic."

"Me too, but I didn't know you felt that way."

"Who didn't?"

"Do you still?"

He laughed. "I fell a little in love with my own version of her. I never really knew her. By the time your letter caught up with me, about her with someone else—was it Jules Raleigh?"

"Yeah."

"By the time I got it, I was in Denver. I was glad I'd made the whole thing up and didn't have to come back to someone real. I could never be like Movie Star. I could never trust a girl enough to let her stay now that I'm this wrecked:

a cripple, a deafie, shrapnel lodged in me like lice in a stray dog's fur."

"Don't make it worse than it is," I said.

"He wrote me, you know. Mr. Raleigh wrote me."

"I didn't know that. When you were in the Gulf?"

"No, later. I was in the hospital. He was already kicked out of here."

"He wrote you from Vermont?"

"Yeah. He said he'd heard about the big celebration at Linger, and he was sorry to miss it."

"No one there knows the truth."

"Linger's not about truth. . . . He said something I liked. He said experience is a hard teacher, because you get the test first and the lesson afterward."

"He dumped her, you know."

"I didn't know."

"I don't think he had a choice with Mr. D. on his case."

"Probably not."

I wasn't going to tell him about Mom bringing the boil to a head with the Camel cigarette story. She didn't want me to say anything about it. She was really ashamed of her part in all of it now. She'd finally seen the truth.

But I did tell Bobby that Lynn had returned all his letters to me, and her mother had given me an unopened one that had arrived from the Gulf after Lynn left. Lynn had asked her to.

We were driving very slowly up Highland Hill so we wouldn't run over one of Berryville's own. Everyone who noticed us was waving and calling out Bobby's name, calling out "Welcome home!"

"My letters to her are so dull," said Bobby. "Maybe I could publish them in a book called *War Is Exciting but Are Those Who Fight It?*"

"How about *Letters I'd Have Never Answered Except for the War?*" I shouted so he'd hear me. He had a lot of trouble hearing.

They weren't very funny jokes, but we were both laughing hard. I think we were glad things almost seemed the same with us; the war hadn't changed that.

It was good to see Bobby slap his knee laughing.

Sometimes the expression on his face was so dark, I wished there was a way he could put some of it into words, and that it'd help him to have me listen.

But when he was like that, I knew enough to leave him alone.

I can tell you something about yellow ribbons. I hope I never see another one. They were like an invasion of canaries flapping on every tree limb as we drove into Linger.

I knew who'd have to take them down, too.

The B.H.S. Marching Band was playing "Dixie" for no reason I could think of, and about a half dozen tail-wagging town dogs were running through the beds of petunias that had come up red, white, and blue.

"Drive up to the back entrance," said Bobby. "It'll be easier."

He was right. There was no way he could walk through the crowd without people stopping him, or reaching out to touch him, or snapping his photograph.

I saw this beautiful, blond-haired girl in a red dress out by the back steps, and my heart did a flip.

"Did you see her?" I said to Bobby.

"I thought you had a girl," said Bobby, grinning.

"But did you *see* her?"

"I didn't take a good look."

"Now I know why the heart will wander."

"Speaking of wandering hearts," said Bobby, "isn't that Betty Chayka over there?"

"She always asked for you," I said. "Did I write you that?"

We were pulling into a parking place reserved for Bobby when we heard Dunlinger's voice calling his name.

"Himself," I said.

"Yeah, what's with him? He's running toward us like his pants are on fire."

The minute I cut the motor, he was around on Bobby's side, opening the door.

"What's the matter, Mr. D.?"

"You've got to come directly to my office, Bobby."

"What's the matter?" Bobby asked again.

"Just come!" he said.

"Me too?" I said.

"No, Gary. I only want Bobby."

He was hovering over Bobby, as though breathing down his neck would make him move faster.

Bobby was going along on his cane, slowly, his cap tucked into the epaulet on his uniform.

He was letting his hair grow long in back. He said he was going for a ponytail when he got mustered out, probably in September.

I watched them go, Dunlinger's hands moving in the air, as they always did when he was upset about something.

I wandered back up toward the rear steps, and I saw the girl in the red dress again.

I'd never seen her around Berryville, never seen anyone who was even close.

I wondered if she'd come down from Philly for the occasion, and I used that as an excuse to talk to her.

"No," she said, "I'm here with my boy-friend. . . . Wasn't that Robert Peel?"

"He's my brother," I said.

"He's why we're here."

"He's why everybody's here today."

"No. I mean, he's why my boyfriend came from New York. He's inside now—in the owner's office? Have you heard of Gus Sanchez?"

39

The band was playing "Hey, Jude." He came out the back door with Bobby as Amy and I were standing in the sun, watching Gulf, the Dunlingers' new Persian kitten, chase one of the big dogs on her spidery legs.

I held the door for them. Sanchez was first.

Somehow it was worse that it was the face. I remember that I sucked in my breath when I first saw him, and my breath came back in a phony-sounding cough. My heart felt as though it would come through my shirt.

One eye had a black patch. There was not much left of his nose, and part of one lip and his chin were gone. He was in dress uniform, on two canes. Behind him my brother, on his cane, was trying to direct him down the stairs. Amy stepped in to help.

"Here we go," she said; something like here

we go. I saw Bobby's face next, saw him seething, heard him snarl at me, "Gary, get the car!"

"Shall I take him home?"

I was talking about Sanchez as though he wasn't there, and Bobby didn't bother with introductions.

He said, "You're going to take all of us back to the house!"

Then he told Sanchez to wait at the bottom of the steps, he'd be back, and he said the same thing to Amy: wait, be right back.

She called after him, "Don't *you* want to stay?"

Bobby didn't answer. We were walking side by side back toward the Dodge.

"What happened?" I said.

"I've got to get out of here!"

"What did Dunlinger say?"

"He said there's a friend of yours in my office. I think under the circumstances you'd better send him away, Bobby."

"He said *that*?"

"He said he's going to make everyone nervous and depressed, Bobby. I'm as sympathetic as the next man, he said, but you're asking too much of people with this fine young man if you put him on display. And it isn't fair to *him*, either, Bobby, he said, it'll humiliate him."

"Did Sanchez hear this?"

"No. And he didn't hear the part about the seating arrangements being already fixed for the speakers' table, and anyway, how could we expect people to enjoy their lunch, looking at, quote, that poor fella—his face isn't even human anymore, unquote."

"What did you tell him?"

"I told him you're the only thing that isn't human anymore, Mr. D. Don't worry, we're not going to rain on your parade. There won't be any publicity pictures captioned WAR WRECKS LUNCH AT LINGER!"

It was then that we saw Betty Chayka across from us in the parking lot.

She was in blue Spandex pants, and a red-white-and-blue shirt. She had on white high, high, heels with stars and stripes painted on them.

"Hey, Bobby! I been looking for you!"

"Later!" he called back.

I shouted across, "When we get back."

She was holding her bag under one arm, and the hand holding the American flag dropped so the flag hit her shoes. Even from that distance I could see the smile on her face disappear.

When we got inside the car I said, "We *are* coming back, aren't we?"

"You think I'd come back here?"

"Bobby, this whole damn day is about you. Mom and Dad—"

He cut me off. "If this whole damn day is about me, why isn't my best buddy invited?"

"What are you going to tell Sanchez?"

"What *can* I tell him? He's going to know."

"You're right. . . . You're right about everything, Bobby."

"Bobby, he said to me, I planned this entire thing for you. Now don't spoil it, he said. . . . I said you fucking planned this for yourself, Mr. Dunlinger. You know what he said?"

I said, "He probably said don't say that word in Linger."

"Close. He said don't stoop to gutter language, Bobby, not in Linger!"

We got Sanchez and Amy into the back, and we were ready to roar out of the parking lot when Bobby said, "Wait! Stop!"

Then Bobby rolled down the window and called out, "Chike? Chike? Want to come to a party?"

She came running toward us, as fast as she could on gravel, with heels that high.

40

Word got out when Bobby didn't show up that day. It got out over our telephone, where Chike sat for hours while Amy opened cans of Bud in the kitchen and passed them from Sanchez to Bobby to her.

Bobby couldn't hear well on the phone, so he sat on the plastic hassock near Chike, declaring that public relations made everyone so thirsty, copying down the names of newspapers and radio stations from the county yellow pages.

When Chike finished the area calls, Amy started calling the 212 numbers she got from New York City information.

Mr. Dunlinger had a lot of coverage in the weeks to come, not quite the kind he'd planned.

One article in a national magazine was called "Shame on Linger," and when Sanchez appeared

206

on *Oprah*, someone called in comparing Dunlinger to Hitler.

After that Fourth of July in Berryville, Linger was blackballed by most of its best customers.

Even Sloan's father wouldn't patronize the place.

I spent the summer on roller skates, with Sloan, in white pants and yellow shirts with waffles stamped all over them, hustling Waffleburgers down to parked cars.

Sloan kept a scrapbook called Playing Gulf. She collected all sorts of news clips: a picture of General Norman Schwarzkopf singing onstage in Disneyland with Mickey Mouse, and being interviewed with a stuffed bear by Barbara Walters.

There were photographs of the oil-well fires still raging, and one of the emir's triumphal return to Kuwait when it was finally safe. There were reports of the thousands of new Mercedeses shipped there, and of the Egyptians and Asians cleaning Kuwait up, since no Kuwaitis did manual labor. Soldiers from Bangladesh were assigned to seek out dangerous mines, and U.N.

troops from thirty-three countries guarded the borders.

"It's a chicken book, though," she said. "I don't have anything in here about how many Iraqis were killed or what the place is like now."

"All the attention's on the Kurds, anyway."

"I know it. Why is that?"

I quoted a favorite poet:

"Silly old Iraqis, dish towels on their heads, tackiest of tackies."

My father stayed on at Linger.

What do you expect me to do, he said, you want a fifty-five-year-old man who's never done any other kind of work to quit his job in the middle of a recession on principle?

Is that what you and your brother want me to do, he said, put principle over mortgage payments, car payments, and what it's going to cost for Gary to go to college in two years?

I knew he wouldn't be able to resist bringing my college into it.

But nobody asked him to quit.

Even when my mother decided to take a bookkeeper's job at Scheck Fuel, nobody suggested he should look around, too.

At the very end of August Lynn Dunlinger came home. Sloan and I saw her one Friday night, coming out of the movies with Mrs. D. She said that after Le Soleil closed, she went to Montauk to visit her roommate from Faith Academy. She looked pale and she didn't smile. Mrs. D. said, "Well? Tell them who you saw in Montauk!"

For a crazy moment I thought she was going to say she saw *him*.

But she said, "I saw Billy Joel. There was a fundraiser and he was there with Paul Simon and Foreigner."

"How about *that*?" said Mrs. D., all smiles herself.

But Lynn's expression didn't change, and she didn't meet our eyes.

"Are you home for good now?" Sloan asked.

"I got into Dartmouth," she said. "I'm leaving next week."

Then her mother said, "We miss you, Gary," and steered her away, waving a good-bye.

I thought Mr. Dunlinger would never live down that day he turned Gus Sanchez away. But by the time fall rolled around, the traffic was picking up

on Highland Hill. And the weekend they tele-
vised the Clarence Thomas nomination hearings
for the Supreme Court, the bar and The Grill
were jammed with after-dinner drinkers hanging
around to watch Anita Hill and him on the giant
screen.

Mr. Dunlinger hired a young Vietnamese music
student to play in The Regency Room. The
Linger ads boasted of her awards and her talent,
and that she was attending college on a Linger
scholarship.

Linger . . . Linger. It was hard to escape the place
as I went back to school and picked up the old
routine. At Christmas, when Berryvillers hiked
up the hill for carol singing under the trees, I
could hear them from our front porch, and I
could see the tiny, twinkling colored lights in the
distance.

At Easter the children rolled their eggs on the
lawn, and Friday evenings a Teen Night was in-
stigated in a community effort to stop drugs and
drinking among high school kids. Rock stars
were invited to play in the new Young Adult
Room, and early dinner was included in the

price. I'd hear glowing reports from my dad, and finally from Dave and Ollie—everyone was heading up to Linger.

Always the giant American flag waved in the breeze on top of Highland Hill, and again Linger became the focal point for Berryville.

I knew my mother missed being there terribly, and in time my dad began telling her the gossip, recounting stories of the regulars, and Mr. and Mrs. D. And if my mother wasn't there, she *was*, in spirit anyway, at the cocktail hour when my folks would fill each other in on their days. . . . I'd hear the old familiar sounds from my mother: "He said *what*?" and "What did Mr. D. say about that?"

And it was good to hear them laughing and talking together as they always had.

Sloan turned Playing Gulf in for a Current Events project and got a B minus, with a note reading *Provocative but dated, don't you think? We're Current Events, not History*.

The "current" was underlined.

Bobby is in New York City now, looking for work, hanging out with Sanchez and Amy. He left his journal and his letters and tapes with me. He said he didn't care what I did with them. He'd remember, he said, what he'd remember.

When we talk to Bobby on the phone, we don't mention Linger or Mr. Dunlinger.

I say things like How's Chike and he says Well, she misses *you*, how's Sloan?

I say She doesn't miss me, Sloan's fine.

And then he usually asks, "What's going on?"

"Not much," I say. "Things are the same around here."

And most things are.

Sometimes I catch myself singing Mr. Raleigh's song—snatches of it:

> *So linger awhile, let's see that smile,*
> *Secrets are mysteries still. . . .*

There is no word of Jules Raleigh. I still see him in my mind's eye, that afternoon he stood looking down at Lynn in the snowstorm, evenings he'd tuck the violin under his chin and play "Claire de Lune" or sit at the piano to do Simply Red's "Something Got Me Started."

And I see him in class, bobbing toward the chalkboard to write something, underlining it sometimes so hard the chalk would break:

DO SOMETHING ORIGINAL!
SAY SOMETHING PROVOCATIVE!
WAKE UP YOUR PASSIONS!
CHANGE!

And:

FEEL FOR OTHER PEOPLE!